Skies of Fire

Skies of Fire

THE ETHER CHRONICLES

ZOË ARCHER

AVONIMPULSE
An Imprint of HarperCollinsPublishers

EPub Edition APRIL 2012 ISBN: 9780062109149

Print Edition ISBN: 9780062184498

10 9 8 7 6 5 4 3 2 1

To Zack, who makes every day a wonderful adventure.

Chapter One

The skies above the Carpathian Mountains.

THE DECK OF the airship *HMS Demeter* rocked from the force of another concussive blast. The hull took no damage, but the crew lurched like drunkards as they fought to keep the ship steady. A direct hit to the engines from the enemy's ether cannons would send the *Demeter* plunging down over a mile to the jagged mountains below.

"That was a bit close, lads," shouted Captain Christopher Redmond. The din of cannon and deck-mounted Gatling guns nearly drowned out his voice, gone hoarse with yelling orders. "Let's make 'em earn their gulden. Hard to starboard!"

He was loud enough for the crew to hear. Dawes, the helmsman, turned the wheel, and the ship banked sharply to the right, narrowly missing another blast from the Hapsburgs' ether cannon.

Through his goggles, Christopher stared at the enemy ships. Bad odds. Five-to-three in favor of the Huns, and one of the Hapsburg dirigibles was a dreadnought, carrying thrice as many guns. The corvette class *Demeter* was tiny by comparison, only as long as two railway carriages.

A convoy of Russian and British seafaring vessels had been attacked by a Hapsburg airship as they'd traveled across the Black Sea. The *Demeter* and two other British airships were there to respond and had flown to the aid of the convoy. Fighting among the vessels had ranged all the way into enemy territory. Over the Carpathian Mountains, four more Hapsburg dirigibles had joined the fight, resulting in this disastrous battle.

No British reinforcements would fly in to lend support. All he and the other British captains could do was fight, and hope they made it out alive.

Which might not happen. The *Danae* and *Psyche* were taking heavy hits, and, faintly over the boom of gunfire and roar of the wind, Christopher heard the airships' captains bellowing orders to their crews.

"Looks like they're beating a retreat," noted Pullman, the *Demeter*'s first mate.

"Which means we have to do the same," Christopher said. "Damn it." He hated retreating. The Man O' War part of him rebelled at the thought alone. He battled to keep down his impulse to fight—a continual struggle, since the telumium implants that had made him into a Man O' War fed his already strong aggression. Retreat was counterintuitive to men such as he, men who had been transformed into amalgams of flesh and metal.

But sometimes retreat was the only option. Strategy took precedence over gallantry.

He smiled grimly to himself. *Sounds like something Louisa might say.*

The middle of a disastrous battle was no time to think of her, of the curve of her neck or the way she picked her morning rolls apart before eating them in discrete bites. A cunning strategist, his Louisa.

She's not mine any longer. She made her choice.

"Prepare for withdrawal!" he yelled. Right now, he had to get his ship and crew to safety. Perhaps if he survived, he might allow himself a conciliatory dram of whiskey in his quarters, permitting a rare foray into regret and self-pity. A good deal of gunpowder and ether lay between now and then, however.

Turning to issue another command, he paused for a moment, catching a faint whine—a sound undetectable to the normal ear. He threw himself to the deck, taking Pullman down with him. Both men looked up to see a bullet hole in the bulkhead just behind them.

"You'd been any slower," Pullman breathed, "that bullet would've drilled right through your head and mine."

Another reason to thank the telumium implants. The rare metal stimulated his adrenal glands, making him stronger and faster than an ordinary man, and sharpened his senses. He could see the rivets on an airship half a mile away and hear a bullet seconds before it made impact.

The implants also made him a target. If he was killed, his airship would lose its most important source of power—him. The metal plates that were fused with his flesh powered the batteries that ran the engines, a reaction which created the ether that kept the ship aloft. Snipers armed with ether rifles always accompanied airships into combat, counting on the fact that a Man O' War captain was impelled to stand above deck and put himself in the heat of battle. Christopher knew two captains who had been taken out by snipers.

Damned ungentlemanly, the use of snipers. Ten years ago, no naval force would have ever considered such ill-mannered tactics during combat. But ten years ago, the Man O' Wars didn't exist. Warfare, and tactics, had changed since then.

Grabbing his own ether rifle from its mounted scabbard on the ship's central support, Christopher took up position at the rail. He sighted the would-be assassin on the deck of a Hapsburg ship, his enhanced vision bringing the enemy into perfect clarity. After drawing a steadying breath, Christopher fired. Moments later, the sniper dropped.

"Good shot, sir." Pullman grinned as he collapsed his brass spyglass.

"They're all good shots, Mr. Pullman." Christopher jammed the rifle back into its holster.

"Aye, sir."

Christopher cursed when he saw three of the five Hapsburg ships position themselves between him and the retreating British airships. If he wanted to join his comrades in their withdrawal from the battle, he'd have to get through the Huns. Including their massive dreadnought, with its superior firepower. Trying to break through their line would see him and his ship blown out of the sky.

His alternate route didn't look much better. Two Hapsburg ships advanced from the other side, a high rocky ridge behind them. But these airships were smaller frigates. There just might be a chance . . .

"Bring her about, Mr. Pullman," he ordered. "Until we're facing those two enemy ships. And prepare to vent the ether tanks."

"Captain?"

Christopher grinned. "We're going to show these Huns a little British audacity."

After giving Christopher an answering grin, Pullman shouted the order to the venters, who made the necessary adjustments to the large tanks at the back of the ship. They signaled their readiness, and Pullman yelled, "Make ready for venting!" He repeated his command into the shipboard auditory device so the crew below would know to prepare themselves.

Like the other members of the crew, Christopher braced himself, taking a bit of rope from a capstan and wrapping it around his hand. He secured his footing.

The wooden-hulled airship turned, placing her side to the three enemy ships as she was aimed toward two more Hapsburg ships. It was a risky stance to be in, but the *Demeter* had to be positioned for her flight.

He had to time this just right. At any moment, they could be fired upon.

A few seconds more, and then—

"Now!"

The venters threw the levers. Three things happened simultaneously. The *Demeter* dropped lower, a fast plunge of twenty feet. Enemy ships fired, blasting the area where his ship had just been. And the ship rocketed forward, pushed faster by the rearward release of ether from the tanks. Christopher was grateful for his goggles, as brittle wind scoured his face. That had been one of the first adjustments: speed. Even at its slowest, an airship was damned faster than any seafaring vessel, including a clipper. He allowed himself a smile. There was something deeply thrilling about racing through the sky with the velocity and view of a god.

The forest below became a green blur, smeared with gray from rocky outcroppings.

Gravitational force shoved at him as the *Demeter* sped forward, but he kept himself from falling, his legs wide-braced, his grip secure on the rope.

The ship raced forward, right toward the two Hapsburg frigates. Between the two enemy craft was a distance of barely a hundred feet, making for a tight squeeze. If the *Demeter* cleared the narrow space, it would be a feat worthy of a dance-hall ballad.

"Hold straight and steady, Mr. Dawes," Christopher shouted at the helmsman.

Though Dawes had turned chalk-white, his eyes wide behind his goggles, he did as he was ordered, keeping the *Demeter* on course. Some of the crewmen on deck crossed themselves, and a few took out lockets that held photographs of wives and children.

Christopher had no locket with a sweetheart's photograph. As a member of Naval Intelligence, Louisa had been protective of her image, not wanting any record of her face that could possibly fall into enemy hands. When she left him, all that had remained behind were memories and anger. And one kidskin glove. She had a habit of misplacing gloves.

As the *Demeter* sped toward the enemy ships, the spiky mountains just beyond them, Christopher wondered if Louisa would learn about his death in the papers. No—she abjured newspapers.

If there's information I need to know, she had said one afternoon over tea, *I'll ferret it out.*

Do you know what I'm thinking right now? he had asked.

She had smiled, her slow, wicked smile. *I'm a very good spy. And I do enjoy a thorough interrogation.*

An extremely pleasant afternoon had followed. More than a few long, lonely nights patrolling the air had been spent in contemplation of that afternoon. Anger had always been quick to follow his memories. He couldn't think of the times they'd shared without recalling the way it had ended. The empty bed when he'd awakened. No letter, not even a note. She was just . . . gone.

One way or the other, if he didn't survive, she would know. Was it petty of him to hope she'd be saddened by the news? He was a Man O' War—not inhuman.

The ship gained speed, getting closer and closer to the two Hapsburg frigates. Christopher could see the astounded enemy crewmen scurrying across the decks, and the captains—Man O' Wars like him—bellowing orders. They were making the guns ready to fire on the *Demeter*.

"Prepare to return fire," Christopher roared.

The gunners acknowledged the order, and, fighting the force of the speeding ship, readied the cannons. They all stared at him, waiting for the command.

He waited, too. Everything needed to be timed perfectly. Closer. Closer. The *Demeter* was almost between the enemy ships.

"Fire!"

Guns from both sides boomed. The *Demeter* shuddered as some of the enemy fire slammed into the hull, but the ship held strong. The enemy ships also took hits, and Christopher noted with satisfaction that several of their ether tanks and guns were damaged.

The *Demeter* sped through the narrow passage between the frigates. As it raced past, a wake of air knocked into one of the enemy ships. It listed, then thudded into the mountain just behind it. Crewmen scrambled out of the way of rocks tumbling free from the mountainside. One sizeable rock slammed through the deck, scattering men and splinters of wood.

There was no time for celebration, however. The mountain was just ahead. If Christopher's ship couldn't make the crest, it would smash into the massive pile of rock.

Here was one of the times Christopher wished airships were built of metal, like their seafaring ironclad brethren, but wood was far lighter. Airships sacrificed hull strength for the ability to fly.

Christopher raced to the wheel. "No offense, Mr. Dawes," he said, taking the wheel from the helmsman.

"None taken, sir." In truth, Dawes looked relieved that Christopher would assume responsibility for guiding the ship over the dangerous peak.

The wheel in one hand, Christopher grabbed the shipboard auditory device. "Give 'em everything," he ordered the engine crew. "Flank speed!" He hoped that, between the turbines and the venting ether, they'd have enough power to make it over the mountain. Switching the auditory device to shipwide, he shouted, "Everyone, hold tight!"

Just before the *Demeter* crashed into the rocks, he pulled back hard on the lever that controlled the vanes behind the turbines. Gritting his teeth with effort, he fought to keep the airship climbing. The jagged face of the mountain sped past. Cold blue sky gleamed beyond the prow. Crewmen shouted as the ship rose up, almost completely vertical. Every muscle in Christopher's body strained with effort. Even strong as he was, he still had to fight gravity.

Heat sizzled through him as the implants drew on his energy, both feeding off of and building his power. He hadn't liked the sensation at first, the strange symbiosis between him and machinery, but now he reveled in it, knowing he needed as much strength as he could muster in order to ensure this ship and crew's survival.

It might not be enough. They weren't going to make it. The top of the mountain rose too high up. They'd lose power and career into tons of stone, raining wood, brass, and canvas down onto the valley below.

No. By God, if he had to die, it would be in combat against the enemy, not smashed against unfeeling rock. Louisa might claim to value cunning over valor, but his values were different.

Groaning, he pulled harder on the wheel, turning to correct the sudden tilting of the ship. Then—the *Demeter* just crested the peak. Rocks scraped against the keel. The ship juddered. Suddenly, they were over.

And plunging downward. As tough as the climb upward had been, now the ship took that force and rushed down the other side of the mountain. They plummeted into a valley.

Wind tore at Christopher's face and clothes, his coat flapping behind him, as he steered the ship down the face of the mountain and into the heavily wooded valley. With another groan of effort, he pulled back on the vane-controlling lever right before the *Demeter* crashed into the ground. The ship shot forward. Into the forest. He piloted the ship between huge, ancient trees, their massive trunks stretching toward the sky. With the ether tanks vented, the ship didn't have its normal height. Flying low was the cost of their speed.

Had the woods been any younger, there would have been no room to fly the ship. But the forest—what he could see of it past the green, shadowed blur—seemed older than time itself, exactly the place where giants roamed. Christopher zigzagged through the woods, whipping around trees, keeping the ship racing onward.

Even with his precise piloting, tree limbs snapped against the speeding hull, and the crew shielded themselves from falling branches.

"Throttle back," Christopher shouted to the engine crew.

Details of the forest emerged from the blur as the ship slowed. The wooded valley appeared uninhabited, no sign of chimney smoke or a clearing. Wherever the *Demeter* was, the known world—and friendly territory—was far behind.

"All stop," Christopher ordered.

He brought the ship to a hover just beneath the heavy forest canopy.

"No one move," he hissed. "No one speak. Not even a scratch or sneeze."

"Aye—"

"Quiet!"

Everyone, Christopher included, kept still and silent. The shadows of the Hapsburg ships passed overhead. Breath held, he watched the frigates lingering just above. Searching for the *Demeter*. With any luck, the Hapsburgs would think they had crashed, and move on.

Christopher didn't believe in luck. If a body wanted something to happen, only effort would make it come to pass. That's how he rose from a midshipman to a captain in such a short period of time. He worked his bollocks off for it.

Yet he wouldn't mind a dram of luck right now. As

he kept his gaze upward, a drop of sweat worked its way down his back.

Hours passed. Or minutes. But after what felt like hundreds of years, the enemy ships flew on.

He didn't permit himself a sigh of relief. Several more minutes passed as he made sure that the frigates did not return. At last, reasonably certain that they were in the clear, Christopher gave the order to power up the engines.

After guiding the ship toward an open patch of sky, he brought the ship up above the tree line. More mountains lay all around them. Aft of the ship was the battle they had just fled, and presumably the remaining Hapsburg ships. Retracing their route meant the possibility of finding themselves back in combat, and being vastly outgunned and outnumbered. Doubtless the two British ships were already hightailing it back to friendly airspace.

Which meant that the *Demeter* was deep in enemy territory. Alone.

"What now, sir?" asked Pullman, coming to stand beside him.

"We steer clear of enemy ships, fly hundreds of miles of hostile territory, and hope the ship holds together for the journey home." He grinned. "Easy."

The first mate shook his head. "I'm certain Mr. Herbert will enjoy charting that, sir."

"Our navigator enjoys a challenge," Christopher answered. "If he doesn't, he should."

"Aye, sir."

As Pullman strode off, Christopher surveyed his crew. Some of the younger men appeared shaken, but most had recovered enough to go about their usual duties. Good. He relied on a capable and steadfast crew, expecting as much of them as he did himself. If the *Demeter* and the one hundred and fifty men aboard were to have any chance of survival, everyone needed to be diligent and aware.

At the least, this stretch of mountains seemed sparsely populated. Off the starboard side, he caught sight of a tiny village, its sloped roofs forming a scrap of habitation here in the wilderness. The ship's engines would be heard by the villagers, but unless a farmer had a telegraph line directly to the Hapsburg Admiralty, the *Demeter* ought to be safe.

The faint *pop pop* of artillery caught his attention. The sound came from the village. He ought to steer clear of that . . . except why would there be ground military action out here? He'd received no reports of it. Damned strange.

"Some of ours, sir?" asked Tydings, the bosun.

"There haven't been ground battles this deep in enemy territory."

"Maybe a local skirmish."

He hadn't heard anything about internal conflicts, but this was isolated terrain, and it was always possible that native factions were engaged in their own disputes. Disputes that, judging by the sound of it, involved dozens of armed troops.

"If it *is* some conflict between local factions, we'd best stay well away from it."

"Sound plan, sir."

"Glad you agree, Mr. Tydings."

The bosun reddened.

Christopher was about to adjust the ship's course when something gleamed in the village. A shimmering, like light bounced off a mirror. When the glinting happened again, he knew it was not simply sunshine bouncing across a window. It repeated itself. A flash. Another flash, longer this time, and then another. A pattern. Coming from the second story of a barn at the edge of the village.

His senses sharpened further.

"That's code, sir," Tydings said.

"Aye." Someone was signaling—using code belonging to British Naval Intelligence. "A distress call." He made another change to the ship's bearing, steering toward the village.

Whoever was down there, they were allies and needed help. As dire as the *Demeter*'s situation might be, as her captain he was honor-bound to come to the unknown British agent's aid.

He cursed when he saw ground cannons being pulled toward the barn. Once the heavy guns were in position, the British agent would either have to surrender or be blasted into pulp and powder.

"Prepare a jolly boat for landing," Christopher commanded. "I'll need Royal Marines with good aim for the landing party."

"You mean to lead the party yourself, sir?"

"If the man down there *is* Naval Intelligence, he'll want to speak with the captain directly. Don't worry, Mr. Tydings. Anything happens to me, there's enough power left in the ship's batteries and ether in the tank to get you the three hundred miles to the northern border of Greece."

The bosun saluted and moved to follow the order. As the marines assembled, Christopher handed the wheel back to the helmsman.

"Keep us circling, Mr. Dawes. The local army hasn't spotted us yet, and that's how I'd like to keep it." Christopher checked to make sure his rifle was loaded with both ammunition and ether. He tucked an ether pistol into his belt.

Properly armed, he made his way belowdecks. The *Demeter* followed similar configurations of other airships, with charging panels built into many of the bulkheads. They hummed as he passed, generating power from his proximity. Insulated cables ran from the panels, which lead to a central battery deeper in the ship. The ship's engines drew their power from this battery.

After passing the orlop deck, Christopher reached the hold, where seven marines waited beside the jolly boat. The small metal craft had no oarlocks or sail. Instead, an ether tank was mounted on the center bench, and a small turbine was bolted to the stern, with a tiller attached to the turbine. A swivel gun was mounted in the prow of the boat.

At Christopher's nod, the marines clambered into the jolly boat, and he did the same, taking up position at the tiller. Sitting on the benches, everyone fastened leather straps around their waists and buckled themselves in securely.

"We're going to make a quick extraction," Christopher said, "and then get the hell out of there."

Once he was certain they were all well strapped in, he nodded at Dawes, standing beside a tall lever. "Now, Mr. Dawes."

The first mate pulled the lever. The cargo gates opened and the jolly boat plunged downward in freefall.

Christopher had long since grown used to the fall, but two of the marines looked ashen, their lips white, as the jolly boat hurtled toward the ground. He waited until the landing craft had cleared the hull of the ship before throwing the valve that activated the ether tank.

With a jerk, the boat stopped its plummet. It hovered for a moment over the trees until he turned on the turbine. The jolly boat hummed as it surged forward under his guidance.

He steered toward the village, and cursed when, looking over the side of the boat, he saw two dozen uniformed troops surrounding a two-story wooden barn at the outskirts—the origin of the coded signal. Someone on the small second floor of the barn shot back at the soldiers.

As Christopher searched for a place to land, he was careful to keep out of sight of the troops. A wooded ridge stood some quarter mile from the barn. An ideal spot for a concealed landing.

He guided the jolly boat to the ridge, between the trees, then brought the boat down.

"You five," he said, pointing at the marines, "with me. Farnley, Josephson, you stay with the boat. When I signal, bring her to the barn. Farnley will steer as Josephson uses the swivel gun to soften up the enemy during your approach."

"What about the cannon, sir?" asked Josephson.

"We'll just have to get out before they're rolled into position." Lucky that the troops didn't have any draft horses or tetrol-powered engines to pull the heavy guns, or else the timeline would get damned abbreviated.

Knowing that they hadn't much time, he led the marines down the ridge, all of them careful to keep their steps quiet. As they neared the barn, sounds of gunfire grew louder as did shouts in Romanian—a language Christopher couldn't speak, but he knew what *Surrender or die* sounded like in any tongue. The man in the barn continued to shoot, making plain his feelings on those options.

The troops had formed a ring surrounding the barn, and none of them saw Christopher or the marines creep out of the woods. Their attention remained fixed on the cornered British agent. Christopher led his men toward an eight-man section of the encircling enemy soldiers.

Silently, Christopher signaled to the marines to wait for his command. As some of the enemy soldiers paused to reload their weapons, giving him the opening he needed, he gave the signal. They rushed forward.

Christopher sprang, pushing away from the ground in a powerful leap. The troops barely had time to turn around before Christopher descended on them. They stared with wide eyes as he dropped down from an impossible height. He swung out with the butt of his rifle, the force of the blow knocking back two soldiers. They flew back ten feet and sprawled, unconscious, in the dirt.

Man O' Wars seldom fought on solid ground, but when they did the results were always devastating. It was one of the many reasons why they had been created. They were unrivaled weapons who also happened to be men.

Though the marines didn't have implants like his, they were highly trained. They brought down the closest enemy troops, creating enough of an opening in the cordon to rush toward the barn. One soldier lunged to bayonet a marine. A bullet pierced the would-be attacker's chest, and he fell. The shot had come from the man in the barn. Whoever the British agent was, he had damned steady nerves and remarkable aim.

Christopher and the others sprinted toward the barn, fighting off the enemy as they ran. The nearest wall had no door, and dashing around the barn looking for an entrance gave the enemy far too many chances to shoot them.

So Christopher ducked his head and, shoulder-first, rammed through the wall. Planks shattered around him. The barn itself shuddered from the impact but stayed upright.

He barreled ahead, allowing the marines to follow through the hole he'd made. Two of the marines fanned out, quickly setting up a perimeter. The other three entered the barn behind him, then they too joined the perimeter and fired back at the enemy. One covered the hole in the barn Christopher had just made.

He surveyed the barn. A set of stairs led to the second

floor. He heard the footfalls of the British agent above. Whoever he was, he did the intelligent thing by taking a higher firing position. The footsteps were lighter than Christopher expected. Perhaps the agent was a young man, or of slight build.

A pair of feet appeared at the top of the stairs. They wore a woman's buttoned boots, scuffed from use.

The agent walked cautiously down the steps.

Christopher's gaze traveled from the hay-dusted hem of her skirt, up past the slim curve of her waist and the hands that held a rifle.

He cursed.

A pointed chin. Wide-set hazel eyes framed with dark lashes. Dark brown hair tumbled over a high forehead. He knew exactly what that hair felt like, its sandalwood fragrance as it spread across his pillow, remembered how pain had lanced him when the scent faded. And the sharp stab he felt now was born of pure, unadulterated shock.

"Hello, Christopher," Louisa said.

Chapter Two

LOUISA SHAW STARED at the man she once knew as well as her own heartbeat. It had been three years since she'd seen him. Her last glimpse of him had been as he'd sprawled in bed, asleep. She'd taken one final look—he would have awakened if she'd tried to kiss him—and had slipped noiselessly out of his flat. Out of his life. Forever. Or so she'd thought.

His transformation startled her. Word had reached her that he'd become a Man O' War. She'd met other men who'd undergone the transformation. But none of those men had ever been her lover. None of them had touched her body—or her heart—intimately.

Christopher had been a lanky man. Long legs, long arms. A body more lean than bulky. She used to amuse herself by tracing her fingers along the shapes of his ribs until he could no longer hold back his laughter. Never would she have anticipated a decorated naval captain to be ticklish.

He was bigger now, thicker with muscle. His wide shoulders filled the blue wool of his coat, and his thighs pulled tight against his breeches. God, he'd even gotten taller. She had to tilt her head back further to look him in the eye. The size of him, the strength that radiated from him—judging by the crash and the splinters of wood on his coat, he'd just *run through* a heavy wooden wall—she could hardly believe he was the same man.

His face hadn't changed, though. Still had the same aquamarine eyes, the same angular jaw, the reddish blond hair, now cut very short. The same mouth she remembered kissing for hours. When Christopher smiled, his grin was enormous, dazzling. Now, his lips pressed thin as he looked at her.

She would deal with his hatred later. Right now, she needed to survive this firefight and complete her mission.

The marines that accompanied him were already spread out around the barn, defending their location. Gaps showed in the old structure's walls, just the right size for a rifle's barrel. The report of their guns filled the barn with noise and smoke.

"The Admiralty never told me you were out here." His voice held the same low, gravelly rasp; only when he spoke now, his words were taut. Certainly not flirtatious remarks or husky murmurs of seduction.

"Operatives' missions aren't divulged. Especially when their mission entails going undercover."

"Just what *was* your mission?"

She nodded toward the opening he'd ripped in the barn wall. "We need to get out of here."

"I'm not going to risk your life by running that gauntlet without a plan." He paced through the barn, gaze alert and assessing. "There's a way to get you safely out of here. I just need to find it."

"Command wouldn't send me into the field unless I could handle myself."

"They might be comfortable putting your life on the line." He peered through a gap in the wooden wall. "*I'm* not."

"You aren't in charge of my mission. The decision isn't yours to make."

He prowled toward her. She fought the impulse to back up. *It's still him*, she reminded herself. *No matter what kind of metal has been implanted in his body. No matter if he has the strength of three men or has the means of powering an airship.*

Granted, even the Christopher she had known probably wasn't very fond of her.

I made a decision. It's over and done. All that remains is surviving. Moving forward.

"Tell me about this covert mission."

Though enemy troops ringed the barn, with gunfire everywhere and heavy guns being rolled into position, speaking with him proved to be the most unsettling thing of all. She told herself it was simply because his presence here was unexpected, as was the alteration in his appearance, but she knew all these cloaked the real reason behind her disquiet.

"I'd been undercover for months, getting close to a rumored splinter faction within the Hapsburg regime. There are those within who want this war and bloodshed finished, even at the cost of their country's victory. Finally, I received word that a contact would meet me here and give me vital information. So I came to rendezvous with him. And that's when we learned we had been betrayed."

"Where is he?"

She nodded toward a corner of the barn. Christopher swore when he saw the bullet-riddled body sprawled in the hay.

"The troops showed up just after he gave me the intelligence. Surrender isn't an option, so I tried to fight them off as long as I could." She held up her pistol. "Thought I was going to have to save one bullet for myself. Then I saw the British airship. A damned lucky break, I thought. It was my best chance of getting out alive." What she hadn't known was that Christopher was the ship's pilot. And power source. Perhaps it hadn't been as lucky as she'd first surmised.

His expression darkened. "You don't need to save a bullet for yourself. I'll get you out of here." He moved to the improvised doorway, edging away the marine guarding it, and pulled a snub-nosed gun from inside his coat. Instead of firing the gun at the surrounding enemy troops, he discharged it into the air. A streak of light shot from the barrel. "Our escape route will be here in a moment."

He was only doing his duty. He'd come to her aid without knowing who she was. Their history had nothing to do with his present actions. Yet she was grateful, all the same. It was a cold, rueful gratitude, but there.

"Enemy's field guns are in position, sir," one of the marines said. "They're sighting us in."

Louisa's stomach clenched. They didn't have much time.

A humming sound followed by the rapid pop of artillery snared her attention. It didn't sound like the enemy's guns. She darted around him and took up a position by the hole in the wall.

"Appears our ferry has arrived," she murmured when Christopher joined her. He stood at her back, peering over her shoulder. This close, she felt the tremendous heat radiating from him, and caught the scent of hot metal. Evidence of how much he'd altered.

A jolly boat flew over the treetops. At the prow of the boat, a marine manned a swivel gun, firing it at the enemy. Christopher used his rifle to take down two soldiers, and the boat altered its course, steering closer to where he'd taken his shots. Unable to advance further, the boat landed just beyond the tree line, with the enemy forming an obstacle between the small vessel and the barn. Half of the troops turned their attention toward the jolly boat. The marine piloting the boat quickly took up his rifle and held off soldiers advancing toward the small vessel.

The distinct clank of cannons being made ready rang out.

"We're cutting a path to the jolly boat," Christopher said to Louisa and the marines. "That outbuilding"—he pointed to a small stone structure that stood midway between the barn and the tree line—"will block some of the troop movements. The enemy will be closing in on us, so we've got to be lively."

A huge boom sounded. Louisa crouched as the barn shook. Shattered wood rained down.

Rising up from her defensive stance, she saw a huge hole in the ceiling. Through that hole, she noted that half of the second story was gone.

"Fall out," Christopher called to the marines.

They did as he commanded, one of the marines taking point as Christopher ushered her and the others through the improvised doorway. With his warm hand at her back, Louisa ran full out toward the waiting boat, firing her pistol at the blocking troops as she sprinted. Her peripheral vision caught glimpses of Christopher shooting at the enemy with astonishing speed.

She and the others fired as they ran. As Christopher had planned, the small outbuilding kept the troops from fully closing around them. The gunner in the jolly boat provided assistance. With bullets whining all around her, taking bites out of the earth as they narrowly missed, she kept all her attention focused on holding back the enemy. It wasn't the first time she'd been fired upon, and it would not be the last. She hoped.

They held off the soldiers just enough to slip through the barricade. She followed Christopher as he sped through, aware at all times of the enemy's nearness. The boat was just ahead. Almost there.

The line of soldiers closed behind them. She ran at top

speed, Christopher right beside her. He could run faster. She knew it. Yet he was deliberately slowing his pace to stay with her.

Moments before they reached the waiting boat, two enemy soldiers rushed out from the nearby woods. A marine shot one down, but the other was faster and reached Christopher.

Before Louisa could react, he planted his fist in the soldier's jaw. The man soared back as if a battering ram, not a man's fist, had hit him.

Suddenly the ground disappeared under her feet, and a band of iron wrapped around her waist. Then she was bodily thrown into the boat as if she weighed no more than a grenade.

Only for a moment did she allow herself to lie in the bottom of the vessel, steadying her spinning head. As she did, Christopher appeared at the edge of the boat.

"Get up," he snapped, "and get yourself strapped in."

She scrambled upright and sat on one of the benches and secured the harness. As she fastened the buckle, his hands brushed hers out of the way to finish the job.

"These need to be good and tight." His tense words were at odds with the gentleness of his touch. It had always amazed her that a man with such large, calloused hands could be gentle, and it surprised her even more now. Not only was he still deeply angry with her, he'd also become an amalgam of man and machine. Yet instead of squeezing the breath out of her, he carefully adjusted the harness until she was secure.

As he did, the marines continued to shoot at the advancing troops.

Unfazed by the gunfire, Christopher bent close in order to adjust the buckle. She saw how his skin had darkened in the intervening years, a consequence of being on the deck of an airship, and the small lines that radiated out from the corners of his eyes. Their gazes caught and held. Drawing air became difficult.

She never forgot his eyes, blue and warm as the Aegean. Those waters were chill now. Impossible to swim in them.

But at the heart of those depths, she caught the gleam of remembrance. And longing.

It was gone before she could look closer. He pulled away, and took up position at the tiller. "Josephson, stay on the gun."

The marine at the swivel gun nodded. She was about to offer that she was also trained on such weapons, but the hard set of Christopher's jaw made her decide against it. He was captain, and challenging his command in any way would undermine his authority.

"May I?" she asked, reaching for the ether rifle at Josephson's feet. At his nod, she picked it up and opened the bolt to ensure it was loaded.

She glanced up to find Christopher watching her. "I only had three bullets left."

He gave her a clipped nod. "Everyone secure?"

"Aye, sir," the marines answered, all of them firing at the enemy.

She took aim and shot, pinning the enemy down for the boat to make its escape.

"Aye," she said, then couldn't resist adding, "Kit." That had been her name for him in private, when they'd done relentlessly pleasurable things to one another.

Heat flared in his gaze. Just as quickly, the heat disappeared. He drew his revolver and fired at the enemy troops. One soldier screamed and dropped his rifle to clutch his injured hand.

She could not help but stare. It had been an amazing shot, deliberate and precise as a surgeon's scalpel. But Christopher had simply acted, and seemed well used to performing such incredible feats.

As the enemy troops neared, he steered the boat straight up into the sky.

SHE HAD BEEN on airships before, but never one as small or maneuverable as this jolly boat. Her stomach gave a flip of protest as the boat shot up and turned sharply. The ground fell away. Air and bullets rushed past. She crouched low, her legs locked against the bench, the rifle gripped in her hands, as the marines returned fire.

Christopher kept his hand upon the tiller, his eyes in continuous motion, his expression steely. He looked confident, determined. Difficult to say whether her heart pounded because she flew through the air with Hapsburg troops shooting at them, or because Christopher was *here*, and more devastating than ever.

She would have to puzzle that out later. Right now, she

had to defend the boat and help get everyone to the safety of the airship. The intelligence she had gathered needed protecting, as well.

Leaning over the side of the boat, she fired at the soldiers below. The ether rifle's kick knocked her back slightly, but she steadied herself and continued to shoot. She'd never fired a weapon from a moving airship before. The men and buildings below looked deceptively small, as if this was nothing more than a child's game.

The enemy's two heavy guns were no toys, however. Soldiers pointed them at the boat, and loaded shells into their barrels. The marine manning the swivel gun in the prow of the boat fired at one of the large weapons. It tumbled onto its side, a smoldering pile of metal.

The second cannon boomed. Louisa hunched low as Christopher banked the jolly boat hard, just avoiding the hurtling projectile. Had his skill been a fraction less, everyone in the boat would have been blown from the sky.

As the gunnery crew hurried to reload, Louisa took aim. She winged the soldier loading the shell, chambered another round, and then put a bullet in the leg of the soldier attempting to pull the cord that released the firing pin. The two soldiers went down. By the time back-up soldiers arrived to man the gun, the boat had flown out of range.

As she released the spent cartridge from the chamber, Louisa caught Christopher's terse but approving nod. It oughtn't gratify her, yet it did. He probably didn't think highly of her as a person, and a woman, but he could respect her as an operative.

She only permitted herself a sigh of relief when they were well and truly away from the village—the site where she might have died, had it not been for Christopher. Yet she kept her rifle across her knees, easily accessible if she needed to call it back into service.

With the village and heavy guns behind them, they sped on through the sky. Treetops and jagged mountains below, endless blue vaulting overhead, and wind across her cheeks. The sensation filled her head with lightness. She blinked as the rushing air drew tears from her eyes.

One hand on the tiller, Christopher pulled something from an inside coat pocket, and with a nod in her direction, pressed it into the closest marine's hand. From soldier to soldier, the object made its way to her.

A pair of goggles. Of course Christopher had a supplemental pair on him. He'd always been attentive to the details. In every aspect of his life.

She slipped on the goggles, adjusting the leather straps to get the fit right. They were men's goggles, and a little large for her face, but the relief from the biting wind was immediate.

"Thank you," she shouted above the wind.

His response was to curse with the depth and creativity only a sailor possessed.

She scowled. He might not care for her, but he didn't have to be so sodding rude.

Then she saw that he wasn't looking at her. His gaze remained pinned on something behind her. Twisting around, what she saw made her swear, as well.

An airship skimmed the horizon. Even at a distance,

she recognized its unique lines, with two ether tanks mounted on the underside of the hull. Not a British airship. Hapsburg. A jolly boat with a small ether tank could never outrun a massive ship of the line. Within minutes, it would be on top of them.

The jolly boat dipped, and suddenly they were just below the canopy of the forest. The overhead branches formed a thick covering.

Christopher steered the boat close to one of the trees, finding a wide enough gap in the branches to bring the vessel right up against the trunk.

"Take the tiller, Mr. Farnley." Christopher unstrapped himself from his harness and stood. Facing the tree, he gripped the trunk, then nimbly leapt onto it. In a moment, he disappeared, climbing up the tree as though he was part cat.

She hurriedly unbuckled her harness and rose.

"Ma'am," one of the marines said. "I don't—"

She lifted a finger to her lips, and the marine silenced himself. Carefully, she picked her way down the length of the boat, using the men's shoulders for stability as she moved toward the tree.

Like Christopher, she gripped the trunk, then leapt onto the tree. She climbed upward, weaving around the branches. Just above her, she spotted his boots.

"Get down," he growled, "and stay with the boat."

She continued to climb, until she reached the very top of the tree. Christopher held to one side, and she remained on the other. The tree narrowed at the top, so that a distance of only a foot separated them.

"Damn it, Louisa." His eyes were hot with anger behind his goggles. "You want my help, then you do what I say. Get back to the jolly boat."

"I need this vantage." She nodded toward a nearby range of hills to the north. "The splinter faction has an enclave up there. If the soldiers from the village head toward their position, the whole mission is sunk."

"What *is* the damned mission?"

"We can talk ourselves hoarse. Later. I'm not discussing covert intelligence at the top of a spruce."

Gripping the tree with one hand, she tugged her goggles up onto her forehead. She reached into one of the many pockets sewn into her skirts, then found the object she sought.

The brass spyglass snapped open, and she held it to her eye, gazing toward the hills. "I need to see if the enemy advances on the enclave. If they do, I'll need to warn the splinter faction so they can disperse."

From her high position, she saw the edge of the village and the road that the soldiers would take if they marched toward the hills. Thus far, the road remained clear.

She offered the spyglass to Christopher.

"Don't need it."

Here was more proof he had changed. She stared at him for a moment as he looked toward the village. Same face, same memories. But a very different man. One who could see half a mile away without the assistance of binoculars or a spyglass.

She brought the spyglass back up to her eye. As she

continued to watch the road out of the village, Christopher exhaled.

"Enemy airship's turning away. We're in the clear."

"Not quite." She wouldn't let herself feel relief until she was certain the splinter group was safe. Continuing her surveillance, she looked toward the other end of the village, where the road continued, leading away from the hills.

The bedraggled remnants of the soldiers assembled there. They hauled the remains of the heavy guns behind them.

"Appears as though we've scared them off," she said. "They'll be heading back toward the nearest cantonment, which is about ten miles south."

Lowering the small telescope, she discovered him watching her. Her heart kicked.

It was peaceful up here. Deceptively so, with the wide green canopy spreading around them, and the wind rustling through the boughs. One could almost pretend there wasn't a war happening, and danger lurking behind every cloud. With Christopher so close, close enough for her to see the reddish gold of his incipient beard and the curve of his lower lip, she was inundated by a rush of hungry yearning she had no business feeling. Not the way she'd left things between them.

He opened his mouth as if to speak. Then shut it.

"The *Demeter* will be coming for us," he finally said. Without another word, he began to climb down the tree.

She pocketed the collapsed spyglass and followed.

Anything she felt for Christopher had to be ruthlessly shoved aside—including the way in which his unrelenting coldness made her chest ache.

He was already sitting at the tiller by the time she reached the waiting jolly boat, and watched with detached reserve as she clambered back into the vessel. At the least, he waited until she fastened her harness and put her goggles in place before guiding the boat out of the trees.

They moved toward a rocky outcropping. An airship's prow and figurehead emerged from behind the crag. She tensed, until more of the ship emerged. The top-mounted ether tank proclaimed her to be British.

They approached the airship. Though she was no stranger to the vessels, the sight of these flying ships never failed to stir her. The *Demeter*, as the name upon the hull proclaimed her to be, was a sterling example of the Her Majesty's Aerial Navy. The ship followed the standard British design, with a large ether tank mounted on a central support beam, just beneath the curved wooden dorsal fin running from prow to stern. Smaller ether tanks were also mounted on the fin. A pilot house stood in front of the ship's secondary battery, situated in the aft, and this connected to a massive turbine. All Man O' War ships carried full compliments of weapons, and the *Demeter* had guns both topside and poking through gun ports belowdecks.

As part of her duties, Louisa needed to know the workings and layouts of all naval vessels, including those that flew. Yet, for all her knowledge, the sight of a massive ship of war hanging in the sky still widened her eyes with amazement. And the *Demeter* wasn't simply an unknown Man O' War's ship. It was Christopher's.

She glanced back at him, to find his wary gaze upon her. They both knew precisely the symbiotic nature of his relationship with the ship. It was, in essence, *him*.

"She's bonny," Louisa said above the wind.

The lines bracketing his mouth lessened. "The crew keeps her trim and orderly."

Judging by the cannon-sized holes in the hull, the *Demeter* had been in a firefight not so long ago. Perhaps even today, since the holes hadn't been patched. He'd said nothing about being in combat, but there hadn't been much time for conversation back in the barn.

As they approached the ship, crewmen gathered at the rail and peered from portholes. Doubtless they were curious to know who their captain had just rescued.

Christopher guided the jolly boat beneath the ship's keel. A cargo gate opened, and the boat rose up until it hovered inside the *Demeter*'s hull. Once the boat was inside, a man wearing a first mate's uniform pulled the lever that closed the gate.

The moment the gate closed, Christopher took the rifle from her hands and leapt out of the boat, his movement light and powerful as a lion. When she'd last seen him, he had been exceptionally fit, but now he had a strength that was literally inhuman. He pulled off his goggles and began talking in a low, quick voice to the first mate.

She unbuckled her harness and stood. Disembarking from a hovering jolly boat proved to be more challenging than anticipated, the vessel unsteady beneath her feet. Louisa cursed as she toppled forward.

And found herself snug in Christopher's arms. They pressed chest-to-chest, her hands braced on his shoulders, his palms splayed on her back.

God, he was so warm, his sharply handsome face so very much the same. They had embraced just like this many times, though always in private, for they had each been protective of their careers and reputations.

He shifted his hold to clasp her with one arm. She felt the brush of his calloused fingers over her face, a gesture so oddly tender it made her heart flutter. Her gaze flicked down to his mouth. It didn't matter that a complement of marines and the first mate stood nearby. She just wanted to feel him again, taste him . . .

He moved his hand yet upward, and tugged. She blinked. He'd simply taken off her goggles. No tenderness there, only the removal of some gear.

Yet as he lowered her to the ground, his movements were slow. Deliberate. She slid down the length of his body, aware of every inch of solid muscle beneath his uniform. As he seemed aware of her body, his fingers briefly clasping her waist before releasing her.

He stepped away. Turning to the first mate, he said, "Mr. Pullman, escort Miss Shaw to my quarters."

"Aye, sir. This way, if you please, miss."

Louisa faced Christopher. "Where will you be?"

"Consulting with my navigator," he answered. "We're deep in enemy airspace and need to find someplace safe to make repairs."

"I'll come with you."

His gaze frosted. "It's safer in my quarters."

"If I wanted safety," she replied, "I would've taken that clerical job at Admiralty headquarters. You know that. Besides," she added as he began to object, "I know this territory. I can tell your navigator where the least inhabited and patrolled areas are."

He narrowed his eyes. For a moment, the cargo bay was silent, save for the humming of the engine. The marines and first mate looked back and forth between her and Christopher, watching the silent battle. The mess would hear some enthralling tales tonight.

Without a word, he turned on his heel and strode from the cargo bay. She hurried after him.

As they moved up through the ship, she noticed lengths of copper tubing running along the bulkheads, like metal veins. From studying airship schematics, she understood that the tubes carried ether from the batteries mounted throughout the ship. The ether was an accidental, but important, byproduct created as the batteries transformed Christopher's energy into the means to power the ship. He wasn't merely the ship's power source, but also its way of staying aloft.

The first time she'd met a Man O' War, she had been leaving a debriefing at Admiralty headquarters. Captain Daniel Kerrick had been walking in just as she was exiting Admiral Porter's office. Even though she was difficult to rattle, she'd been awed at the size of Captain Kerrick, and how he seemed to radiate barely leashed power.

Since then, she'd encountered others of the man-machine hybrids. There was always an element of danger surrounding these men, a sense of the uncanny. After all, they weren't ordinary men, but men who had telumium implants grafted to their bodies, who had strength and sensory capability far beyond that of normal humans. They commanded and fueled airships. Difficult not to think of them as monstrous.

But she had met those other Man O' Wars only after they had undergone their transformations. She had known Christopher, in every possible way, when he had been simply a man.

Though Christopher had never been *simply* anything. *Don't think about that now. Don't think about what you walked away from. All that matters is the mission.*

She repeated this over and over as she followed him and his astonishingly wide shoulders through the ship. Curious crewmen appeared, giving her respectful salutes and murmurs as she passed. But they weren't curious simply because of her gender or her role as an operative. She could see their speculation. Wondering what her relationship with the captain was, or had been. Shipboard gossip moved faster than a hurricane.

The crew would have quite a lot to talk about. Yet this far behind enemy lines, she just hoped the force of the past didn't tear her or Christopher's ship to pieces.

Chapter Three

SHE TRAILED AFTER Christopher until they reached the navigator's room. Charts, maps, and equipment covered every available surface. The young lieutenant saluted as they entered. Like everyone else on the ship, he barely hid his inquisitiveness at her appearance.

"Your findings, Mr. Herbert," Christopher said without preamble.

The navigator snapped to attention. He pointed to a section of the map spread on the table before him. "We should find a safe pocket here, sir. It's far from towns of any real size, and the mountains should keep us screened from the enemy."

"There's a military installation in that area," she said. "Five hundred troops, and they've got ether cannons, so you wouldn't be safe from bombardment. However," she continued, pointing to a different stretch of mountains, "this region is all but uninhabited, and what populace does live there are poor peasants with no access to telegraph lines. If my airship were damaged and I needed someplace to drop anchor for repairs, that's where I would go."

Mr. Herbert glanced at Christopher, uncertain.

"Your intelligence is reliable?" Christopher asked.

"Of course. *I* gathered it."

The corner of his mouth threatened to curve upward. Once, long ago, when they had been watching the night sky from the warmth of his bed, he had confessed that he found her confidence enthralling.

Not maddening? she had asked. The night had been cold, especially with the balcony doors thrown open to better see the stars, and she and Christopher had snuggled together beneath a fur blanket taken from a captured Russian ship.

D'you think I joined the Navy because I want an uncomplicated life? It's challenge that I want. And challenge you give me.

Ready for another challenge? She had rolled atop him, straddling him, and pinned his wrists to the bed. *Try and get free.*

He had grinned, that wide, spectacular grin that never failed to captivate her. *Get free? Why would I want to?*

A sharp throb of loss resonated through her now, as she and Christopher stared at one another across the map. It seemed an appropriate measure of the distance between them—the map and its depiction of thousands of miles.

"Give Mr. Herbert the precise coordinates of the installation and the isolated area," he finally said.

She hid her exhalation of relief, then told the navigator precisely where to avoid and where to find the safety she had described.

"Have everything you need, Mr. Herbert?" Christopher asked, once the lieutenant had finished transcribing her notes.

"Aye, sir."

"Come with me, Miss Shaw." Hardly had these words left his lips than he paced from the navigator's room.

She struggled to keep up with his long-legged stride. He had the advantage of knowing not only the layout of the ship, but the movement of the crew, so he neatly wove past crewmen going about their duties without breaking pace. Her mouth firmed with determination. If he sought to make her feel awkward, he'd have to do better. She moved just as nimbly, skirting past crew carrying equipment, never hesitating when the companionways seemed a complex maze.

She'd spent long hours poring over the schematics of every airship in Her Majesty's Aerial Navy. Including the plans of the *Demeter*, knowing full well that Christopher was its captain. She had pictured him walking the decks, direct and unfaltering in his pace. Or she'd thought of him in his cabin, reviewing his log and absently rubbing at his jaw, as he always did when he read.

Of course, when she'd thought of him then, he'd looked the same. Whipcord lean, quick to smile. Not the man he was now.

Knowing the schematics of the *Demeter*, she understood without being told when they approached his quarters. He pushed open the door, startling the cabin boy. The young crewman stopped in the middle of picking up books scattered across the floor.

"Dismissed," Christopher said, entering the cabin. She immediately followed.

The boy saluted and hurried out, closing the door behind him.

She and Christopher were alone.

He paced to a heavy cabinet and pulled out a bottle of whiskey, then poured himself a glass. After downing it all in one swallow, he poured out another measure and held it out for her.

She took the glass, noting how careful he was to keep their fingers from touching. Uncertain what to say or where to begin, she sipped the whiskey, feeling its welcome burn. As she nursed her drink, she examined his quarters. They were located in the aft of the ship, with a long window running the length of the cabin. There was the carved cabinet, a desk, and a narrow, solitary bed. All standard issue. Much as she'd imagined it.

But she saw that the books the steward had been gathering were not all treatises on naval policy or advancements in shipbuilding. Bending down, she picked up a book near her feet and smiled.

"Still chasing birds," she murmured, holding the book open to an illustration of a song thrush. He had never kept specimens, only watched the birds in the wild. It seemed a shame, he'd said, to admire a living creature and then shoot and stuff it. Or worse, cage the poor thing, depriving it of the open sky.

He stepped forward and plucked the book from her hand. "Tell me what you're doing here."

"Same as you. Fighting to keep the Hapsburgs from claiming the world's supply of telumium." Should the Hapsburgs acquire all the source of the rare metal, found only in a few remote places, they would construct a fleet of Man O' Wars capable of conquering every nation, from Britain to the Americas and beyond.

She finished her whiskey, needing its courage to say what she must, then set the glass down. After taking a breath, she said, "And now I need your help."

An immediate refusal sprang to Christopher's lips. Force of will kept it back, however. For all her audacity, Louisa wasn't foolish. She wouldn't ask for help unless she truly needed it.

If she hadn't spotted his airship, if he hadn't been there to see her distress signal, she would be dead. Either from enemy gunfire or by her own hand. His implants kept him from reacting to cold, yet the thought of her sprawled in the dust, dead, was a bitter chill.

Men who were selected to become Man O' Wars underwent thorough testing to ensure they had strong willpower and self-control. They needed it, for the implants amplified emotions.

Seeing Louisa again, hearing her voice, and even, God help him, touching her—he needed every ounce of his self-discipline to keep himself from sinking into a vortex. Anger, fear, desire. He felt them all at once. Yet he knew in the depths of his heart that what he felt now had nothing to do with his implants.

It was her. She'd always brought out feelings in him, feelings that a lifetime of naval discipline had all but beaten out of him.

And she was here now, on his ship, seeking his help.

"To complete your mission," he said. It wouldn't be for anything else. "Which you still haven't disclosed to me."

"Before we were surrounded, my contact gave me this." She gripped the hem of her skirts and lifted.

Two choices: look away like a frightened prude, or torment himself by seeing her legs. Self-preservation had never been one of his qualities.

Her dark wool stockings hid her bare flesh, but the shape of her legs beguiled him. Louisa's legs were long and sleek, temptingly muscled, the limbs of a woman seldom at rest.

He'd first seen her, and her legs, one night at the Admiralty's ball. He'd been a sea captain back then, with the Man O' War program in its earliest stages. Having grown up at sea, he hadn't yet thought to look toward the skies.

At the Admiralty's ball, however, his attention had been fixed solely on the terra firma. On Louisa. Compared with the officers' wives and daughters, she had been a restless flame, more electric than the recently installed lights. She had been different from the other women who worked for the Navy, as well. Those women seemed compelled to conduct themselves with an excess of gravitas and spoke in quiet, restrained voices.

In her sapphire silk gown, Louisa had circled the

room, her gaze alert, an intriguing half-smile playing about her lips. She had watched the dancers waltz to the clockwork orchestra as though observing the rituals of primitive animals.

"Who is that?" Christopher had asked a fellow captain.

"Louisa Shaw. Intelligence operative. Surprised to see her here. She never comes to these little fêtes." The other man shook his head. "Don't bother, Redmond. Every man who asks her to dance winds up cradling his stones and howling for mercy. Metaphorically."

Even if Christopher hadn't been instinctively compelled to go after a challenge, resisting the allure of Louisa Shaw would have been impossible. He'd crossed the width of the ballroom, steering around the mechanized servers handing out flutes of champagne, until he had reached her. Women often appreciated the sight of him in his ball-dress uniform, but, given that almost every man in attendance had been wearing ball-dress uniforms, he hadn't been able to rely on that advantage.

At his bow, the first words from her had been, "What makes you think you'll be any more successful than the others?"

"None of them is me." He had offered her his arm.

She had laughed, a rich, low sound that made every man with functioning hearing and a pulse turn and stare. She had taken his arm, and together they had walked onto the dance floor. He'd felt the strength of her, then, as they danced, how she moved with a swift feline power.

But others at the ball hadn't been as graceful. A lieutenant and his dancing partner had collided with them, sending both Christopher and Louisa crashing into one of the mechanical servers. Champagne had spilled across her skirts.

He'd growled at the stammering lieutenant, but Louisa had merely smiled and walked away. He had followed her out onto a night-draped balcony.

"There are maids in the retiring room," he'd offered as she brushed at her skirts. When it came to commanding warships bristling with weapons, he was entirely confident. He'd been in the Navy since he was a boy. He knew everything about ships and maritime warfare. A woman with champagne staining her gown, however, was a conundrum.

"Serves me right for coming to this blasted ball," she'd said without anger. But when she lifted her skirts to examine the damage, revealing those gorgeous legs, shock and heat had pulsed through him. Seeing how he stared at her, she laughed and let go of the yards of silk. He'd all but howled his disappointment at losing sight of her legs.

"I spend too long out in the field," she'd said. "It makes me forget rules like 'Don't show a stranger anything below your waist.'"

"Depends on the stranger," he had answered.

She'd laughed again, and he had been lost.

Now he pushed these memories out of his thoughts. Or tried to. But the vision of Louisa lifting her skirts for him threatened his control. Even if he hadn't been a Man O' War, his need to claim would still pound through his veins.

From a pouch strapped to her thigh, she pulled out a piece of folded paper and handed it to him. The document was warm from being pressed close against her.

"Plans for a military structure," he noted after unfolding the paper.

She lowered her skirts, thank God. "A munitions plant."

He spread the document out on his desk. "If the scale of this drawing is correct, the plant is enormous."

"It's the major supplier for Hapsburg munitions. Which is why I was sent to destroy it."

"It would be impossible for one woman, or man, to destroy this structure."

"My contact was going to give me the plans, then take me to a secret faction who'd help me build and carry in the necessary explosives. The Hapsburg troops took exception to our collaboration," she added dryly.

"Did they ever find out the nature of the intelligence your contact gave you?"

She shook her head. "Someone informed on us but only told the soldiers that two spies were in the vicinity. This intelligence," she said, pointing to the plans, "remains active. And my mission is ongoing. I need to destroy this plant."

"Thus the request for my assistance."

"With the major supplier of munitions obliterated, this could turn the tide of the war. Save hundreds, if not thousands, of lives. There could finally be peace."

"No need to convince me. I don't live for war."

"Despite all your . . . changes?" she asked quietly.

"It's my body that's altered. Not my soul."

Now that he had said it aloud, the fact sat between them like an unexploded bomb. Silence stretched out. She gazed at his shoulder, where his implants had been surgically grafted. All Man O' Wars had their implants located in their left shoulders. Minute telumium filaments were attached to the undersides of the implants, weaving into their flesh and encircling their hearts.

"When?"

"Two-and-a-half years ago."

Six months after she had left him. They both knew it. "Because of me."

"The procedure took seven hours, and none of it could be under anesthesia." He forced out a laugh, but inwardly winced at its bitterness. "You broke my heart, Louisa, but not enough to drive me into the arms of that agony."

Her face paled. "I didn't know the operation took so long, or was so painful."

"It's not information that's readily supplied. They only tell you after all the tests and screenings. Almost no one opts out."

"Certainly not you." He didn't miss the faint note of pride in her voice, nor how his pulse kicked in response. Damn it, he didn't want to take pleasure in her respect. He didn't want to feel anything when it came to her.

Telumium implants made him strong—yet they did nothing to protect his heart.

"I wanted to serve my country," he answered. "Half a day's pain meant little in comparison with what would be gained."

"But what was lost?" she whispered.

"You've got no bloody right to ask that," he snarled. He stalked to the window and watched the rough mountain peaks passing below the ship like stone waves. The lowering sun set alight the very tops of the mountains, as though rock could burn. The beauty of the scene touched him not at all. His awareness was confined only to this cabin, and the woman within it, whose voice and face and form conjured up old hopes.

He'd thought the wound had healed. All it had done was crust over, leaving the injury to fester and poison his blood. Only now, with the wound opened again, did he realize how deep the sickness went.

Her footsteps were light upon the floor as she approached him. Light and wary.

"Tell me more about this munitions plant." He turned and strode past her to the table, then stared at the plans.

For a moment, she did not speak, and he waited for her to try to take up the thread of their too-intimate conversation. Yet instead she moved to stand beside him and said, "Very little, outside of what this plan tells us."

"The location?"

She exhaled. "Unknown. The faction my contact was taking me to, they would've led me to it. All I have to go on is drawn here."

Bracing his hands on the table, he studied the plan. "This only shows one wall."

"They'd never build such an important structure out in the open. Too exposed, both to the elements and to the enemy." She planted her hands on her hips.

"This diagram could be incomplete."

"An operative gave his life to make this drawing. He wouldn't have left anything out."

"Except the rest of the walls."

"Unless . . ." She pulled a pair of spectacles from her pocket, then set them on her nose. She looked at him with curiosity, light glinting off the lenses. "No remarks? Jibes about me getting old or looking like a data-scroll archivist?"

"I'd never disparage a data-scroll archivist."

She gave him a sour look and returned her attention to the plan. He sure as hell didn't want to admit that he liked her in spectacles, how they framed her face and gave her a scholarly appearance that contrasted alluringly with her windblown hair and sleek curves. No, he wouldn't admit any of this outside of his own traitorous thoughts.

"Perhaps," she continued, studying the drawing, "this illustrates the single *constructed* wall, but not the others."

"If they weren't built, they have to exist somehow."

"They could be naturally occurring."

"Such as a forest or—"

"A mountain."

Her eyes gleamed behind the lenses of her spectacles. "A fortress, carved right into the side of a mountain."

"Making it impregnable, even to airship attacks."

She slapped her hands on the table, as she often did when excited by an idea. Did she even know she did it? "The perfect location for a munitions plant. Well hidden, easily defendable, all but indestructible."

"Then we've two tasks ahead of us," he said. "The first: ascertain the plant's location."

Nodding toward the window, and the mountains beyond, she said, "A challenge, given the size of the territory. But it can be done."

He'd always admired that quality in her—the utter confidence that she would accomplish even the most insurmountable endeavor. She refused failure, just as he did.

"The second," he continued, "is finding a way to actually destroy the site."

"Clearly, it's heavily fortified." She traced the line that delineated the perimeter. "There's only one way in. This wall will be thick, and protected by armaments, both ordinary weapons and, I'm guessing, ether cannons. Once that wall is breached, it would be a matter of finding the proper location to plant the explosive."

"Fighting off enemy troops all the while," he said. "And there will be hordes of them."

"We won't be able to *fight* our way in. It's impassable by force."

"How else are we supposed to get inside?" he asked.

"Not through an overt fight. Stealing into places is what I do best. Which gives us a better chance of getting in. Getting out, however . . ."

"There's no getting out. No means of withdrawal." He straightened and held her gaze. "It's a suicide mission. But you already knew that."

"It's almost certain that the plant will be too heavily

fortified to make a retreat possible—I only need your ship to get me close," she added. "The rest I can do on foot."

He scowled at how easily she dismissed the idea of her own death. "On your own, trekking in a heavy explosive and then sneaking through their defenses is impossible."

"I'll find a way—"

"You won't. You're a damned good spy, Lulu, but you can't do this. Not alone."

Hell. He shouldn't have called her that. Her pet name, a name she had permitted only him to use in their most private moments. He'd started calling her Lulu as a jest because it didn't suit her in any way—a girl's name, coy and precious—and then it stuck, in the strange backward logic of intimacy.

Intimacy that had been lost. Because of her.

Her eyes widened at his use of her pet name. But this was quickly replaced by anger. "Don't question my ability to carry out this mission. The Admiralty sent *me* for a reason."

She had a point, damn it.

"If this mission is so critical," he said, "I'm coming with you."

"Absolutely not." She knotted her hands into fists. "Whatever you think of me, I'd never want you hurt."

Covert operative she might be, yet there was no hiding the sincerity in her eyes, or the rasp of her voice.

"If I said no, if I set you down here," he waved toward the twilight-steeped mountains, "would you continue on with the mission?"

"Of course," she answered immediately. "This mission is imperative."

"Then I'm accompanying you."

"Kit, no." She stepped around the table and clasped his wrist. This touch alone sent a wave of longing through him, so potent he nearly groaned aloud. All this time, all this hurt, and he wanted her still.

He pulled away. "Unless you've been promoted, I'm the highest-ranking officer on this ship. The decision as to where she flies is mine."

They stared at one another. Both he and Louisa had wills stronger than steel. Neither would bend. He could only wonder which of them would break first.

HE PUT IT to the crew. The final decision was his, but if the mission's outcome meant certain death, he could not discount their opinion.

Crewmen now crowded the top deck, and those who either could not fit or could not be spared from their duties listened in via the shipboard communication system.

Full night had almost fallen, but they couldn't risk being spotted below, so the sodium lights remained unlit. The crew formed a large, shadowy mass as they listened to Christopher, standing in front of the pilot house, explain precisely what the mission would entail. Louisa remained off to the side, near an auxiliary ether tank, watching him as much as the crew's response. She wore a spare coat against the chill, provided by the steward, but it seemed to swallow her with its size. She looked far younger, far more fragile, than he knew her to be.

"There may be survivors," Christopher said, pitching his voice so it could be heard above the wind and turbine. "There may not. We can't count on it. All we can rely upon is that we have a chance to do a great good for our country. A chance to end this war quickly. If it means the sacrifice of my life to ensure the lives of thousands of others, I'll do so, and gladly."

No one amongst the crew spoke, not a murmur, not even a cough. Every man remained motionless, quiet as the depths of the ocean.

"It's a high price, one's life. And one that not everyone is prepared to pay. We all of us sign on to the Navy knowing we face danger, knowing that every time we say farewell to those on the shore, it may be the last time we ever see them. But there is the possibility of death, and then there is the assured truth of it. I'm asking each of you to step toward that future with your eyes open."

Though darkness had settled over the ship, his enhanced vision enabled him to see the faces of his crew, men young and old, orphans and those with family in abundance, as they contemplated what he proposed. Fear, acceptance, eagerness—he saw all of this, and felt it, too, emanating from the decks below. One hundred fifty souls, each of them his responsibility.

"Now is the time for you to decide—will you give everything for your country? Will you ensure the safety of your families, and the generations to come? Or is the cost too dear?"

More silence, until a young midshipman asked, "If it is, sir, what then?"

Some troubled muttering followed from others in the crew.

"If it is," Christopher said, and the muttering died at once, "then the *Demeter* will put you ashore here. You'll have to find your own way home, and I cannot guarantee you won't fall into enemy hands, but you'll be relying on yourself, not me, to make your choices."

Shocked sounds from the crew, and Louisa covered her mouth, but he still caught her soft gasp of surprise.

"Ain't that desertion?" someone else asked. "Sayin' we do make it back home, we'd be court-martialed. Hanged, maybe, or thrown in prison."

"Anyone who opts to leave will carry with them a letter from me, absolving them from charges of desertion or mutiny. Whether the court will take such evidence into consideration, I can't say, but I'll do what I can to minimize the repercussions."

Another wave of muttering rose up. The master at arms stood ready, should anyone turn raucous, but the crew only debated amongst itself.

Christopher glanced at Louisa. She stared at him, arms clasped around herself. Her hair blown into wild disarray by the wind, in her oversized coat, she was an unknown in this realm of airships. It had been his world these past years, a world entirely separate from her, save for the memories that wrapped in thick abundance around his heart. They were wholly discrete, the *Demeter* and Louisa, for he wasn't the same man with one that he had been with the other.

Here she was, however. Watching him with wide, attentive eyes as he tasked his crew to either abandon ship or proceed on a mission that might cost them their lives.

As the captain, and a Man O' War, he could never abandon his ship. They were bound together until the breath left his body and he was nothing but cold flesh and metal.

Louisa was walking—flying—toward her own death. The thought made his insides curl and shudder. And filled him with a bitter irony. She had exploded back into his life with only days left in hers.

He must keep his attention fixed on the mission. Only think of attaining his objective. He'd been living from commission to commission these past years. Now must be no different.

"Those who wish to leave," he said, breaking through the crew's debate, "step forward now. If you're below, come topside. This will be your one chance to turn back. After this moment, we push on and help end this war."

He waited.

Aside from the wind, complete silence blanketed the ship. Not a crewman moved. His acute hearing strained to listen for any crew moving up from belowdecks. Machinery clanged, and someone adjusted a valve on an ether tube. Other than this, there was no motion, no sound.

A minute passed, and then another. No one stepped forward. Some even took a step back, as if to distance themselves from the possibility of abandoning the ship.

Pride swelled within him, and he let them see it in his face. "Good men. The crew of the *Demeter* has bollocks of steel. No one can argue otherwise."

"That's the truth of it, Captain," someone shouted.

"We make it back to Portsmouth, I'm buying a round for everyone at The Cormorant."

"Even me, sir?" asked a boy, second class, a lad no older than fifteen.

"You'll get lemonade. With a shot of whiskey."

The boy grinned, and a cheer went up, even from the men below. He felt their determination resonate through the planks and metal, stronger than the engine or the metal grafted to his skin.

"To your posts," Christopher said.

As the crew dispersed, Louisa drifted toward him. Her movements were purposeful yet lithe, that unique combination that only she seemed to embody. He held himself still as she neared.

She stood close so that only he could hear her. "That was . . ." She inhaled. "Remarkable."

"My crew knows its duty to its country."

"It's *you* they're loyal to. No one wants to let you down." She lowered her gaze, staring at the brass buckles that ran down the front of his coat. "A terrible thing, disappointing you."

His jaw tightened. "I expect only what I know someone is capable of."

"Or what you want them to be."

"They have a choice."

"Why?" She looked up at him, and his greedy gaze took in the contours of her face, the line of her jaw, the curve of her mouth. She was not, in the strictest sense of the word, beautiful, her face more handsome than pretty, yet whenever he looked upon her, his heart clanged to a stop. "Why would you give them that choice? Other captains wouldn't concern themselves with the thoughts and feelings of their crew."

"This ship isn't a democracy. I command it. But I can't drag these men toward death without allowing them to make their own decisions. And this way, having given them the choice, they'll perform to their utmost."

"You were always an extraordinary man."

He glanced at his shoulder. "The implants make me extraordinary."

She smiled faintly. "You didn't have the implants when I agreed to dance with you."

Reminding him of that long ago night acted as an electrical shock, jolting him to awareness. Of the future, and the past. Of regrets and things that would never happen.

"Go below." He turned away. "Temperature drops fast on deck after dark. You see most of the men have beards—it's to keep their faces warm."

"Yet you're clean-shaven. Or were, earlier today."

He scratched at his jaw, bristles already coming in. "Don't feel the cold as much. The implants keep me warm." Bodily, at any rate.

Despite his command to head belowdecks, she moved

past him to stand at the rail. She made a straight, slim figure, silhouetted against the darker mountains.

"Careful." He moved quickly to stand beside her. "The rail's a dangerous place on an airship. One strong gust of wind and you could be thrown overboard."

Despite his warning, she gripped the rail. "So it's not just a plunge in cold water I have to fear."

"You can swim, but you can't fly."

Hardly any lights flickered below, and those that did were tiny, isolated. Above stretched the dark blue bowl of night, stars as bright as wishes.

Yet his awareness was only of her, the pale shape of her hands upon the railing, and the dark tendrils of hair that blew across her cheeks.

He felt as though the tempest itself stood beside him at the rail—unpredictable, devastating. When no shelter was available in a storm, you had to just ride it out.

"At night," she said, "it's difficult to tell how far up we are."

He did not take his gaze from her or the line of her profile. "Even I wouldn't survive the fall."

Chapter Four

THE EVENING MEAL at the captain's table was a tense one. Difficult enough with the ship limping toward a place of relative safety so they could complete repairs. Their pace was slower than usual as the ship cruised low, close to the mountains so they could stay as unseen as possible. No one was much in the mood for pleasantries or storytelling, aware at all times that if an enemy airship should cross their path, the *Demeter* wouldn't be able to truly defend herself.

Having Louisa at Christopher's table, however, made dinner even more strained.

He tried to keep his attention fixed on the excellent roast partridge and potatoes set before him. Duffy the cook prided himself on setting a fine table for the officers. But the food tasted like pasteboard and coal dust. Over and over, his mind repeated, *She's here. She's sitting at my table.*

Hardly anyone spoke as they ate.

Until, at last, Pullman broke the silence. "How long have you been behind enemy lines, Miss Shaw?"

"I'm not at liberty to discuss the specifics." From the corner of his eye, Christopher saw Louisa offer the first mate an apologetic smile. "Suffice it to say that I've spoken more English today than I have for months."

She'd always had a gift for language. Her mother, he recalled, was Italian Argentine, though he'd never met the woman. Louisa had grown up speaking English, Spanish, and Italian. Yet those were only three of the many tongues she knew.

His hands tightened around his cutlery as he remembered all the wicked things she used to whisper in his ear late at night. Even when he didn't know the language itself, he'd known its intent.

"Shall I fetch you another knife and fork, sir?" asked Vale, the steward.

Glancing down, Christopher realized that he'd bent the cutlery into twisted shapes. Damned strength. He needed to keep aware of it at all times, especially now.

He felt Louisa's shocked gaze on him, and his face heated. The other officers at the table also stared. As well they should. Always he'd been careful with what the Navy termed his *amplified potential*—or what he called his *bloody great strength*—keeping himself firmly restrained so no one was accidentally hurt. His losing control was a sight none of his crew had yet witnessed.

Simply having her aboard his ship was a threat. But the mission took precedence over his own wellbeing.

"I've got it." He wasn't interested in performing like a

circus attraction, so he held the knife just underneath the table and straightened it out. The same service followed for the fork.

Another awkward silence descended as everyone resumed eating. The only sounds came from the hum of the engines, the footfalls of crewmen, and the clink of knives against plates.

Louisa took a sip of wine. She made a small hum of appreciation. "This wine is excellent. Grüner Veltliner?"

"One of the spoils taken from a Hapsburg dreadnought. We'd engaged them in the skies above Luxembourg." Young Lieutenant Brown beamed proudly. "Captain Redmond gave 'em a drubbing even their grandbabies wouldn't forget."

"Did he, now?" A smile warmed her voice.

"Aye, ma'am. Didn't look too good for us at the beginning. Dreadnoughts are damned—I mean extremely—big. Far bigger than a destroyer like the *Demeter*. But the captain, he wouldn't back down. Got us to fly *under* the Hun ship, and we softened up the hull. When they were limping, he led the boarding party himself. Faced off against their captain. It made quite a sight, I can tell you. Man O' War against Man O' War." He whistled. "Like one of them battles in a Greek myth."

"Mr. Brown," Christopher growled. "Miss Shaw only asked about the wine. She doesn't want to be bored by your prattle."

The lieutenant reddened, turning his chastened gaze to the table. "Beg pardon, sir."

"I found Lieutenant Brown's recounting of the battle

fascinating," Louisa said. "By the time I learn the details of most engagements, they've been whittled down to the driest, most bureaucratic language imaginable. Naval dispatches don't attempt to compete with serialized novels." She glanced around the table. "I don't suppose anyone on board has a serialized novel I might borrow? My reading material has been sorely lacking since I've been undercover."

Immediately, several officers offered the use of their personal libraries. Taking a drink of wine, Christopher fought the urge to roll his eyes. Having a woman on-board, especially an attractive one like Louisa, could turn the most battle-hardened sailor into a babbling boy.

In his case, her presence turned him into an angry, snarling beast—not the man, or commanding officer, he wanted to be.

"What of you, Chris—Captain Redmond?" she asked. Her fingers curved over the top of her wine glass. "Have you any books I might borrow?"

"Planning on doing much reading, Miss Shaw?"

"Only if I need help sleeping."

An unfortunate picture of her in his bed sprang into his mind. She'd never needed much sleep, and had kept him busy into the early hours of the morning.

"There's nothing on my bookshelves that would appeal to you."

She raised her brows. "I didn't know that your telu-mium implants gave you the ability to read minds. How else might you know what stories I want to hear or what books might interest me?"

The men seated around the table stared back and forth between Christopher and Louisa, fascinated by this exchange.

Bloody hell. He needed to control himself.

"You're welcome to any book, of course." He reached for a platter of more roasted partridge and dished several servings onto his plate. "Except my personal log. That I keep under lock and key."

"Never tell a spy something is locked away." She smiled. "We treat it as a dare."

God—how he wanted to smile back.

Instead, he returned his attention to his food. Louisa and the other officers chatted politely about mutual acquaintances in the Navy, and at her urging, Dr. Singh, the ship's surgeon, recounted the plot of a popular clockwork melodrama that had lately played at the Gaiety Theater in London. She laughed at all the comic parts and slapped the table approvingly when the villain of the piece was apprehended. By the time the dessert of pears poached in brandy had arrived, Christopher felt ready to combust.

So many damned memories. And the longing . . .

He dragged in a breath. This was unacceptable. He was a grown man and the captain of an airship. More important, he was the captain of an airship deep behind enemy lines. He needed to master this, for the sake of the mission. And his own sanity.

When the plates had been cleared, he cleared his throat and stood. "Miss Shaw, grab your coat. I want you to join me topside."

She raised her brows. "Why?"

Right. He needed an explanation. "Your fieldwork in the area can fill in gaps in our charts."

"Is that an order, Captain Redmond?"

"Please," he said belatedly.

The officers assembled around the table all gazed at her, seemingly eager for her response. And when she rose, every man got to his feet. "Five minutes," she said. "I'll meet you there."

He made a stiff bow in Louisa's direction and strode quickly from the room.

On the top deck of the ship, with the cold wind in his face, he felt some degree of control return. He greeted the sailor manning the helm and paced along the deck, hands interlaced behind his back and eyes on the stars.

He knew without turning around that she had come topside. His sensitive hearing detected her footsteps, but more than that, he had a vivid awareness of her at all times.

"Christopher."

Turning to face her, he watched her approach, and he was grateful for her heavy coat's oversized fit.

"Your invitation was unexpected."

He exhaled roughly. "The implants. They . . . stoke emotions. Things dwell closer to the surface, and it can be difficult to control myself." His palm scrubbed over his closely shorn hair. "Usually I can keep a tight rein, but you . . . challenge my restraint."

"It's not my intent to rile you."

"Yet you do, simply with your presence."

"Would it help if I said that your presence riles me, too?"

He snorted. "Not much of a balm, no. But that's why I asked you to join me here. It would do us both some good if we got used to each other. Desensitize ourselves. We can develop a callus, so that there aren't any blisters."

"You're likening me to a foot," she said drily.

He hadn't thought of that, and gave a brief, rueful chuckle. "It wasn't my most flattering analogy," he acknowledged. "The intent remains the same. Acclimatization."

"Very logical of you."

"I'm trying to be." God knew he didn't feel logical whenever she was near.

She inclined her head. "Let us develop our calluses. Shall we walk?"

"Not going to offer you my arm, though."

Now it was her turn to snort. "I always hated that custom. As if a woman didn't have strength enough to walk without leaning on someone, lest they topple to the ground like a collapsed soufflé."

In a kind of amity, they began to walk side-by-side. He nodded at several crewmen as they went about their nighttime duties.

"Can't make a decent meal out of a soufflé," he said.

"Certainly it wouldn't be enough for a Man O' War." She sent him a sideways glance. "You took three servings of partridge and four helpings of potatoes. And I've a feeling that, had there been more, you would have eaten that, too. I remember that you always had a good appetite, but it's increased. Because of the implants?"

Direct, at all times. Years had passed, but she was very

much the same. "We require more nutrients than normal humans. I'm almost always hungry."

"And as captain and power source of this ship, no one will argue or complain if you receive more food."

"Admiralty makes special arrangements for the provisioning of airships." He slanted her a questioning look. "You seem awfully interested in the functioning of Man O' Wars."

"Gathering intelligence is engraved in my nature. I used to think about becoming a journalist, but I found spying a more reputable profession."

He choked back a laugh.

"But I confess," she continued, "I've never known a man before he underwent the transformation. Only afterward. I find the changes . . . fascinating."

"Fascinating? Or freakish?" More than a few angry letters had been delivered to Admiralty as well as the *Times*, decrying the "twisted" and "aberrant" use of technology, the combining of man and machine. He ignored those complaints, glad to be of use to his country, but the idea of Louisa believing he was an aberration made his gut clench.

She scowled. "Again, you're speaking for me. When I say that I find Man O' Wars fascinating, that's precisely what I mean. Everything I know of them comes from newspapers and books."

"But you've met others like me."

"One can't be in Naval Intelligence without having dealings with Man O' Wars. Still, there's never a moment when I can ask them questions, discover what it's truly like."

Familiar with the *Demeter* as he was, he knew without seeing that in the darkness she might trip over a cleat. He took her elbow.

She started.

"Easy." He guided her around the cleat, thankful for the bulkiness of her wool coat. It kept him from feeling the warmth of her skin or true shape of her arm. As soon as he'd helped her navigate the obstacle, he released her.

"Don't want your hungry mind to starve," he said.

Her eyes were wide behind her goggles. "Are you offering me a chance to sate myself?"

He lifted his shoulders. "Take advantage of the opportunity. It won't come around again."

For a moment, she was silent. Then, "Can you feel it? The ship using you as its power source?"

"It's a constant hum. Didn't like it at first, but I got used to the feeling." He glanced toward one of the metal panels embedded in the hull. "The telumium implants channel my energy, which is absorbed there and throughout the ship and sent to the batteries belowdecks."

"The batteries that power the turbines that keep the ship in motion." She bent and examined one of the steel conduits running from a metal panel. "These lead to the battery. But where is the ether collected?"

"There are more tubes that run off the battery that connect to the main ether tank, which is how we're able to fly. Surplus ether is collected in additional tanks which are used in our weapons. Ether pistols, rifles, and cannon."

She knelt down to have a better look at the tubing. "Blast these goggles." She pushed them back and fished her spectacles out of her pocket. "Wish I had your night vision. It's too dark to see anything."

"Here." He crouched beside her and adjusted the dial on a small illumination device welded to the panel. A soft green glow radiated out. "These are found on every gathering panel. It's so the crew can perform repairs during the night without attracting the enemy's attention."

The light reflected off her spectacles, hiding her eyes, but he saw her smile. "Clever, these airship engineers."

"They'd better be. Anything happens to the ship, it's not a simple matter of bailing out. A shipwreck looks like a springtime pageant compared with an airship crashing."

She gazed at him. He was still close, so that a distance of six inches separated them. "You were at the Battle of Rouen. I read about it. It must have been . . ." She shook her head. "I cannot begin to fathom what it was like."

"The skies were made of fire. And the ground was aflame." He'd never wipe the images from his mind, and in a way he hoped he never would. Too many good men died that day. He didn't want to forget them, or what they sacrificed in defense of their country. The British losses had been heavy, but the enemy's invasion had been repelled.

She lifted her hand as if to cup the side of his face. But she seemed to think better of it and let her hand fall.

He couldn't tell if he was relieved or disappointed that she didn't touch him.

"That was a dark day for the Navy," she murmured. "We all wore black for a month after."

"The nature of war. Victory comes at a high price." He

stood, and cleared his throat. On that day, in the skies above Rouen, he'd thought of her, just as he had earlier today. Wishing he might see her one last time, despite the anger knotted around his heart. It seemed that imminent death brought out the sentimentalist in him.

"You wanted to ask a Man O' War questions," he said. "Don't squander the chance."

She seemed to understand that he didn't want to speak of Rouen, or what it meant, any longer. After a last examination of the metal tubing, she removed her spectacles and replaced her goggles, then rose.

They resumed their walk. She asked, "Did Dr. Rossini know that the byproduct of channeling Man O' War energy was the creation of ether?"

"Pure chance," he said, "or so I heard. Still, her discovery didn't go unexploited."

"Allowing for the creation and use of fully-manned, armed airships. Elegant."

"Lucky."

"But useful." She peered at him, and even in the darkness he felt the closeness of her scrutiny. "I don't see it."

"See what?"

"Your *aurora vires*."

"No one can," he said. "Not without a pair of spectral goggles."

"Have you ever looked through them?"

"A few times." Anticipating her question, he said, "Everyone looks as though they have a glow surrounding them. Different colors for different ratings. Green for

Lameth. Blue for Gimel. Golden for Aleph." The *aurora vires* had been Dr. Allegra Rossini's first discovery. Its living energy existed within all people to varying degrees of intensity. She had also been the first to learn how to channel that energy using telumium, leading to the creation of the Man O' Wars.

"What was your rating?" Louisa asked. "Wait—don't tell me." She stopped walking and turned her full focus on him.

There had been many a happy evening when he'd been the subject of her intense concentration. Standing here with her now, knowing she gazed at him so intently, his already hot blood warmed even more.

"Aleph," she said at last. A man needed a rating of Gimel or higher to be considered a likely candidate for the transformation.

He frowned. "How'd you know?"

"It doesn't take a pair of spectral goggles for me to see how extraordinary you are."

A few words from her and his damned heart knocked against his ribs, like a beast eager to please its master. "Admiralty ought to send you scouting for new candidates." He forced his voice to sound light, unmoved by her praise, and he resumed his pacing of the deck.

She caught up with him. "My dance card is already full. There's always another mission."

"So there is."

They were quiet together for a few moments, and he allowed the night and the wind to speak for him. They were surrounded on all sides by darkness, the vastness of the sky, and the shadowed shapes of the mountains below.

"Peaceful up here," she murmured.

"A deceptive peace. You know those lengthy stretches of quiet at sea? They don't last as long up here. An airship travels faster than a sailing ship. The battles and engagements come more quickly. We've always got to be ready."

"Understood. I won't be lulled into complacency."

"As though you could ever be complacent."

She made a soft, rueful sound. "My gift and my failing."

It struck too close to the core of their separation. Yet the tendrils of their old intimacy had already begun to wrap themselves around him. She had always been easy to talk to. And though he knew no good would come of it, he couldn't make himself offer an excuse and walk away.

"Everyone has both," he said. "Natural talents and innate weaknesses."

"I thought a Man O' War had no weakness." They had reached the prow and stood next to one another, staring out at the earth and sky.

"We're not immortal. Nor invulnerable. We heal faster than normal humans, can take more damage, but we're made of the same flesh, the same bones. And we can't be apart from our ships for too long."

Rather than look out at the passing landscape, she faced him. "I never heard about that."

"A small flaw in the good Dr. Rossini's design. These panels," he said, tapping one beside him, "draw off the energy concentrated by the implants. But if any Man O' War spends too long away from them, all that energy within them builds up. It needs an outlet. Otherwise . . ." He shook his head.

"What happens?" she prompted.

"A berserker rage. We lose control. Destroy everything around us, sometimes even ourselves."

Her eyes widened. "Has that ever happened to you?"

"No, thank God. But I've seen cinemagraph images of some of Rossini's early experiments. The men . . . they aren't human any longer." Of course, he hadn't been informed about this particular side effect of the transformation until after he'd agreed to the procedure. He'd been shaken, but his resolve had held. He had wanted to serve his country in the best way he knew. Besides, he didn't plan on being ashore for long. Nothing to keep him there.

"I wonder if anyone could survive it."

"Some have. But the damage they wreak is beyond comprehension. I'm careful, though, to keep that from transpiring."

"You aren't scared that might happen?"

The conversation was getting too intimate. One of hazards of toughening the skin meant there would be rawness at the beginning.

"It's a difficult thing for me to give up control."

"I remember," she said with a smile.

Ah, God, so did he. The battles they had waged for dominance. A hungry, hurting need roused within him. His traitorous hands yearned to hold her.

Go on, then. Want her. Lean into it so it has no power over you.

"So long as I have a means of siphoning off the excess energy, I've no cause for worry." He rapped his knuckles against the wooden rail. "Keeps me sane, the *Demeter* does. She and I need each other."

"Few relationships have such balance." Sadness threaded through her voice.

"An engineer can construct perfect symbiosis." His mouth twisted. "That's where science trumps the human heart."

"I've often wondered if engineers could build a mechanical heart," she mused. "Some kind of clockwork device that sits in the middle of our chests. To keep it running, we just have to wind it with a little golden key we keep hanging from our necks. We'd feel nothing. Only chug along like automatons. Save everyone a goodly amount of pain." Her words were light, yet her expression was bleak.

He wondered—did leaving him hurt Louisa the way it hurt him? There was no good answer.

When she tugged her coat closer, wrapping her arms around herself, he seized the diversion.

"You're cold. It's time to get you below."

"What about the calluses? I haven't developed mine yet."

"Nor I. But that's how this process works. We keep hammering at it until the desired results are achieved."

"By all means," she said, arching her eyebrow, "let's *hammer* away."

He clenched his teeth. Commanding an airship with a crew of one hundred and fifty men offered little difficulty, but commanding his own thoughts—and tongue—whenever she was near proved impossible.

With more of the crewmen watching, he and Louisa crossed the deck and went below. He was grateful that none of the men had hearing as acute as his, or else shipboard gossip would be aflame with intelligence. Already they talked about him and the mysterious Miss Shaw. At all times he conducted himself with constant awareness. He was their captain, and a Man O' War. Friendship and vulnerability were impossible if he was to serve them well.

"You're taking me to your quarters," she said as he walked down a passageway.

He reached the door to his cabin and opened it. Peering inside, he said with surprise, "This isn't the gunnery."

She gave him a look that said she wasn't impressed by his sarcasm. "Why have you brought me here?"

"Because this is where you'll be sleeping for the remainder of the mission." It struck him again that there was every chance the *Demeter*, and everyone aboard, wouldn't survive the mission. He couldn't let himself dwell on it. All he needed to focus on was ensuring that the mission was a success. Living through it was incidental.

She stared at him. "That isn't a good idea."

"It's a fine idea," he countered. "This is the biggest cabin in the ship. Plenty of room for you to go over the intelligence you've gathered. Mr. Herbert can bring you charts so you can compare them with the map of the munitions plant." He gathered up an armful of books from atop the table and shoved them into the bookcase. "There. All the space you'll need."

"We've enough trouble as it is," she said. "It's just asking for more if we share your quarters."

He started. "Bloody hell. You think I . . ." He swore again. "Good God, *no*."

Her caginess transformed into irritation. "You needn't sound so revolted by the idea."

One of the restraints holding him back snapped. Stalking toward her, he said, "*Revolted* isn't the word I'd use. Part of me thinks I should just toss you onto my berth and show you how much I hated you, how much I missed you."

"Ah," she said softly. He nearly growled when her gaze strayed to the berth in question, narrow, but capable of holding two people—if they were wrapped around each other.

He fought for restraint. "But I'm not going to. I'm going to have this ship repaired. I'll find that munitions plant. And then I'm destroying it. Those are the only goals I'll allow myself."

"*We*," she said. "*We* are going to find and destroy the munitions plant. The responsibility isn't yours alone."

"I know it isn't."

She gazed down at the space between them. "I can find another cabin. Bunk with the rest of the crew or"— she exhaled—"sleep in the mess."

"I'd never allow that. You're a guest aboard the *Deme-*

ter, and you'll be treated as such. But don't think that three years have altered the way I feel about you. They haven't. My heart isn't mechanical, and the damned thing still wants you."

Color flooded her cheeks. She opened her mouth to speak, but before she could he turned and left the cabin.

Chapter Five

LOUISA ASSUMED SHE wouldn't sleep well. Her assumption was correct.

She lay in Christopher's bed, surrounded by his familiar scent. Night after night, he stretched his long body out on this same bed and thought of her.

I should just toss you onto my berth and show you how much I hated you, how much I missed you.

His words echoed through her mind all night, tormenting her with images she had no right to see. She remembered their last night together with aching clarity. The feel of him over and within her, the taste of his skin, the sounds of pleasure he growled and the moans he coaxed from her. Those memories had kept her warm over the past cold years, but there had always been a dart of ice at their center, believing that she would never see him again, and when she did, he would likely hate her.

In that, too, she hadn't been wrong.

Restless, she rose from the berth. Wearing only her

chemise, she padded to the window and watched the dark forms of the mountains unspooling beside her.

What a vast world this was. Vast and dangerous. Yet the greatest threat came from herself.

All this time, she had thought she had acted in the right. He would see his error, and be grateful that she had prevented what would have been a catastrophic mistake. It became a mantra she had repeated in the quiet, solitary corners of the night, when regret took advantage of the stillness and howled like a wounded animal.

I made the correct choice. I did what was best. He'll see that.

It had been a fragile fiction, and one easily destroyed the moment she saw him again. *Yes!* her heart and body cried whenever he spoke, whenever he was near. *You bloody fool, throwing this away.*

Could they have endured, had she stayed? Would their feelings for each other have soured, as she had believed, trapping them in ceaseless pain? Or might they have found harmony?

No way to know. She'd seen to that.

Far below, a solitary light gleamed. A cottage, perhaps, or a farm. Dawn approached, and a farmer might be at that moment grumbling and rousing himself from his bed to tend to his early morning duties, with his wife shuffling into the kitchen, yawning, as she readied a pot of coffee for when he came inside and needed warmth. These were isolated and impoverished homes. They wouldn't have the latest in household apparatuses—clockwork coffee brewing devices, mechanized bread toasters. If a cold farmer wanted a hot breakfast, his wife made it for him.

Louisa was no farmer's wife. Christopher never expected her to be.

The only thing that helped hold her regret at bay was his anger. A clean emotion. If he hated her, there could be no room for anything else. But it was worse, so much worse, knowing that he felt more for her than hatred. She'd seen the heat and need in his eyes, and, God, the same hunger gripped her—it had ever since she saw him in that damned barn.

The vibrations of the engines resonated through her bare feet, up her legs, settling in her belly. The engine drew its power from Christopher, and what she felt wasn't the engine, but *him*, his energy and strength, reverberating through her secret places.

She pressed her hand beneath her navel, fighting arousal. There were clever doctors who had built cunning devices, some of them powered by steam or operated by a hand crank. Louisa herself had experienced one of these devices and had found the experience to be . . . extraordinary. With her feet bare, her body attuned to the vibrations of the airship, attuned to *Christopher*, she felt herself excruciatingly aware of sensation.

A wry smile curved her mouth. Doubtful that he'd appreciate being told his massive flying ship of war was, in fact, a device for easing hysteria.

Resting her forehead against the cool glass, her smile faded. Three years ago, making Christopher grin had been so easy. He could be serious, but he'd also been quick to laugh. Back then, he would have laughed at the idea that an airship was a huge vibrating hysterical paroxysm machine.

She'd always loved his laugh. Especially drifting over her bare skin. Would she ever feel that again?

Enough. Other things demanded her attention. Including constructing an incendiary device, evading enemy airships, locating the munitions plant, and then destroying it. And if she and the crew of the *Demeter* survived, so much the better—but survival seemed unlikely.

Yet, out of all of these many, many variables, none of them was keeping her awake. Her restlessness had one source, and she occupied his cabin.

She walked back to the bed, then pulled off the blanket. Wrapping it around her shoulders, she grabbed one of the chairs and set it next to the window. She perched there, knees up, chin propped on her knees. Thus ensconced, she awaited the sunrise.

STILLNESS WOKE HER. She wasn't aware that she had fallen asleep until she found herself in full sunlight, her neck knotted and stiff. Wincing, she got to her feet.

Beyond the window, the sky shone a crisp, unforgiving blue. She observed the serrated peaks of mountains, sparsely dotted with evergreen trees. There were no curls of smoke from chimneys, no roads. This remote section of the Carpathians was too impassable even for the hardy locals to access, which made it an excellent place to repair a damaged airship.

The engines were not running, and beneath her feet the ship felt very still. The turbines might have stopped, but the crew was busy. Men's shouts and the pounding of hammers replaced the engines' hum.

Glancing at the clock on the bookshelf, she cursed. Ordinarily, she never slept past six. Here it was, nearly nine, with the whole of the ship busy and her lying abed as though on a luxury steamer.

Technically, she wasn't *abed*, since she had been sitting in a chair, but the principle was the same. She pulled on her clothes, fighting a groan caused by her stiff muscles, then located a small mirror in the top drawer of a table.

Her appearance was appalling. Face pale against the dark tangle of her hair. She'd seen better-looking specimens on the anatomist's table. Her fingers served as a comb as she dragged them through her snarled hair. Nothing to be done for her ashen skin, however.

If the captain of this ship had been anyone other than Christopher, she wouldn't have cared tuppence how she looked. She was a spy, not a fashion etching. Her appearance had nothing to do with how she performed her duties, especially in these less-than-glamorous circumstances.

But the captain *was* Christopher, and she was honest enough to admit her vanity where he was concerned.

His quarters boasted the luxury of a water closet and a sink with running water. After taking care of her needs and splashing water on her face, she left the cabin.

The ship buzzed with activity. She dodged crewmen bearing planks and buckets of nails. One airman carried a high-powered riveter, with a young man hefting the tetrol tank as he followed. As she walked, the crew greeted her respectfully, tugging on imaginary forelocks. None of them had hair long enough to curl over their foreheads. Having battled her own long hair in the winds topside, she could see the wisdom of keeping one's locks closely shorn.

Finding the galley proved an easy feat, having studied the schematics as well as following the scent of fresh coffee. Heat from the large, dial-covered oven filled the chamber.

"Good morning, ma'am." The cook, standing by a mechanized mixer, smiled, and his weathered face pleated like an accordion.

"Good morning, Mr. . . ."

"Duffy, ma'am." He elbowed the boy winding a clockwork spit. "And this here's Fitzroy."

At Louisa's smile, the cook's boy reddened and mumbled before turning back to his work.

"I know it's late, and I've likely missed breakfast, but I was wondering—"

Before she had finished her sentence, a warm roll and enameled cup of coffee were pressed into her hands.

"Ah, bless you, Mr. Duffy." She took a sip of the coffee and felt herself reborn.

The cook shook his head. "Captain Redmond, he thinks I don't know how to treat a visitor. 'Make sure you set some food aside for Miss Shaw,' he tells me. *Three times.* Don't I run the finest airship in the fleet? Depend on it, we see a goodly share of combat and not too many guests, but I'm no Army cook. I know how to behave like a gentleman."

"And you cook even better than the Emperor of Venice's personal chef."

"Oh, you're a fabulist." Duffy's already rubicund face turned even redder.

"It's true. I've sampled dishes from the Emperor's own table—without his knowledge, of course—and nothing compared to last night's partridge."

"If I didn't work my crew so hard, Mr. Duffy would have them all fat as guinea fowls."

Louisa spun to find Christopher standing in the doorway of the galley. Seeing him in the light of morning, wearing his long, buckled coat and tall boots, her heart pitched like a ship on a storm-tossed ocean.

If *he* didn't sleep well, it didn't show. He looked just as handsome as ever, though his beard had come in a little more, red gold gleaming along his jaw. He hadn't been able to get to his razor that morning, because she'd been in his cabin.

Warily, she scanned his expression. Ever since they had accidentally encountered each other the day before, each moment bore a fraught tension. He'd all but slammed from his quarters the previous night. Did that strange alchemy of hate and desire persist into the morning?

His feeling may have continued, but all she saw in his gaze now was cautious reserve. As though uncertain what either of them might do—anything between a throttling and a kiss.

"Begging your pardon, sir," Duffy said. "But I think

you work me hardest, keeping that furnace of yours well-stoked."

"No engine ever had less complaint about the fuel." Christopher strode into the galley.

She had plenty of opportunity to move out of his way, but her sluggish feet did no such thing. When he grazed past her, his heat was more powerful than the oven at her back, and that faint scent of hot metal replaced the smell of coffee. A moment too late, she murmured something inane and stepped out of his path.

A muscle tightened in his jaw as they brushed against each other. The galley became impossibly small.

And then the moment was over. Duffy handed Christopher a meat pie with a caution. "Careful, sir. Right from the oven and hot as blazes."

"It takes a lot to burn me, Mr. Duffy." Yet Christopher's gaze was on her as he spoke. In four bites, he wolfed down the pie then chased it with a mug of cider. Brushing a scattering of crumbs from his sleeves, he said, "I'm glad to have found you, Miss Shaw. We have a considerable amount about the mission to discuss, and I didn't relish the idea of chasing you all over the ship."

"The search wouldn't have been that difficult," she said. "There's only so many places I could go."

"You can be elusive when you want to be."

She deserved that. "I forget, on occasion, where the job ends and my own life begins. A habit of mine that wants correcting."

After a moment, he gave a small, tight nod. "Will you come with me?" He gestured at the door.

She bolted down the last of her coffee and ate her roll quickly. Glancing up, she saw all the men staring at her.

"Didn't know ladies ate like that," the cook's boy said.

"Fitzroy!" Christopher snapped. At the same time, Duffy smacked the back of the boy's head.

"Your pardon, ma'am."

She only laughed. "I'm a field operative, not a lady. When I've got thirty seconds to eat my dinner before the guards resume their patrols, I can't afford social graces."

After handing her empty mug back to Duffy and thanking the cook for an excellent, if brief, breakfast, she and Christopher walked back toward his quarters. They passed yet more men busily working to patch the ship.

"How long will the repairs take?"

He looked grave. "She took some bad hits to her hull, and a few of the ether tubes need to be replaced. The engines are struggling, too. I'd give it until tomorrow morning, at least."

"Damn. This is a good spot for repairs, but the longer we stay in one place, the greater the likelihood that we'll be spotted—either by an enemy airship, or someone on the ground. It's hard terrain, no confusion about that. But nothing is certain, especially where war is concerned." Nothing was certain where *anything* was concerned, yet she didn't give voice to that.

They reached his quarters, and she followed him inside. The cabin boy had already been through, since the berth was tidily made and the chair moved back from the window. She exhaled in relief. She didn't want Christopher to know how restive her night had been.

As he walked to the table where the plans for the munitions plant were spread, something caught her attention.

"Those are different boots from the ones you wore yesterday."

He glanced down. "The heel had started to come off, so I changed them."

"When?"

"Hmm?" Bracing his hands on the table, he returned his focus to the plans.

"When did you change your boots?"

"This morning," he murmured absently.

"When I was still in here."

This got his attention. "You were asleep. I didn't want to wake you."

Which meant he'd seen her slumped in the chair by the window. For some reason, knowing that he had clear evidence of her disquiet made her uncomfortable.

"Thought about carrying you back to the bed, but I knew you'd be suspicious when you woke up in a different place."

"Ah. Well." She struggled for something, anything, to say. "Thank you." She moved to the table and stared hard at the plans, as if she could lose herself in their mysteries.

"Louisa," he murmured.

She glanced up, and felt herself transfixed with the vivid blue of his eyes, brighter and deeper than the sky outside.

"I didn't sleep well, either," he said.

"Perhaps we need to develop a drinking habit."

"There isn't enough rum."

She drew a breath. "Christopher—"

But it seemed he had reached the limit as to how much of their history he was willing to discuss. He said, "These plans indicate a substantial structure. One of the main factories for munitions to the enemy."

Talking about enemy weapons-manufacturing was a less explosive topic. "Precisely why it needs to be destroyed."

"A building this size," he mused, "carved into the side of a mountain. Doesn't seem that many locations would fit the pattern." He scratched at his chin. "A munitions plant needs to deliver its finished product. There'd be train tracks leading right to it. We need only find those tracks and follow them to our target."

"The factory is in a remote location, but those tracks must head into the industrialized parts of the territory. The *Demeter* would be flying over heavily populated areas."

"May as well paint the target on her hull ourselves." He muttered an oath.

"I might not be able to deliver us right to the plant's door," she said, "but I do know of a chain of mountains, about a day's travel from here via airship. The mountains we're skirting now aren't substantial enough for the plant, but any one of those peaks might conceivably house a giant munitions factory. No bull's-eye on the hull required."

"Can you give the coordinates to the navigator?"

"Of course. I can pilot the ship, too, if you like."

His grin came so suddenly, so unexpectedly, that it felt like a shock of electricity coursing through her.

"*Demeter* is mine. If anyone's leading her to strike at the enemy's heart, it'll be me."

"Hungry for glory?"

"For victory. With me at the wheel, our chances soar."

This time, she was the one who couldn't stop her smile. "Spoken with humility, as always."

"Do you think you could do better?"

"Afraid to find out?" she countered.

He planted his hands on his hips, revealing the ether pistol he had strapped to his waist. "You've never piloted an airship before."

"But I have taken the wheel of an ironclad, and a cutter. Can't be that different."

He outright laughed, and the sound was a velvet glove stroking across her skin. "Naval Intelligence must draw their ranks from the greatest minds in the nation. Either that, or the criminally insane."

"A combination of both works best."

"Spoken as one of Intelligence's finest. But the ship is mine."

"I concede," she said with a wave of her hand. "Only because you're so bloody stubborn. We'd be at this all day."

"*I'm* stubborn?" He laughed again. "This from the woman who, when she was denied entrance to view the Duke of Gorham's erotic automata collection because it might offend her genteel sensibilities, broke into his London mansion in the dead of night, just for a peek."

"My memory fails me." She tapped her finger against her chin. "Yet I seem to recall you were very appreciative of the private tour. Not a word of reproof against me. Perhaps one or two at the beginning of the escapade, but assuredly not when you saw that Indian automaton, the one demonstrating postures from the *Kama Sutra*. That one seemed to pique your interest."

They had, in fact, been so overcome with desire, they'd very quietly enacted a few of those postures, right there on the hand-knotted Oushak carpet. Images inundated her now, remembering their fevered urgency, their partially-clothed bodies illuminated only by the pale blue glow of her quartz torch.

The very same images had to be engulfing Christopher, as well. His breathing roughened, and his cheeks darkened.

"We're equally culpable." His voice was a rumble.

"In that, at least." She, herself, sounded breathless. She was acutely conscious of the nearby bed, of the tension between them, and the omnipresent press of shared history. "A morally suspect spy and an impossibly tenacious airship captain. Who better to steal into the depths of enemy territory and destroy what they desperately need?"

His gaze continued to hold hers. "I'd say we're the perfect lunatics for the job."

THE OBSTACLES IN their path were numerous, dangerous. And enigmatic.

Locating the munitions plant was one such hurdle.

Conquer that, and there stood another: How were they to raze the factory?

Louisa balanced on the rear two legs of her chair, her heels propped on the table. "What are the *Demeter*'s armaments?"

"Sixteen six-inch and four fourteen-inch guns. Four Gatling guns mounted topside for closer combat." Christopher paced around his quarters. He'd shed his coat, and in his shirtsleeves and waistcoat she could see even more the changes the Man O' War process had wrought on his body. His fine white cotton shirt pulled against the hard muscles of his arms, and the dark blue wool waistcoat and its brass buckles emphasized both the breadth of his shoulders and the tapering narrowness of his waist.

When he turned away as he paced, she indulged herself and took a good look at his arse. Snug wool trousers cupped what had to be the most delectably firm backside she'd ever seen.

Good God, she was no better than a stevedore leering at the girls selling oysters.

But, oh, she'd liked digging her nails into his arse when he was inside her, urging him on, feeling his thrusts. Would it be different now, with the transformation he'd undergone? More aggressive? Rougher?

She bit her lip. That sounded heavenly.

Unaware of her thoughts, he continued, "The crew has access to ether rifles and pistols, as well."

"What about . . ." She cleared her throat, her voice having gone raspy. "What about aerial bombardment of a target on land? Is the *Demeter* equipped to drop bombs?"

"We're capable of loading and unloading cargo, but that's it." He crossed his arms over his chest and scowled. "D'you mean to say that there are other navies that actually use such heinous practices?"

She shrugged. "This is war. Technology evolves faster than morals."

"Let's hope Britain doesn't descend to that kind of barbarism. I didn't join the Navy to play Lord Destructor on high, leveling troops or, God, killing civilians from some comfortable, removed distance." He made a noise of disgust.

"Whether you or I agree with the ethos doesn't matter. That kind of warfare is almost here. In fact"—she tipped forward, bringing the front two legs of her chair back down onto the floor with a bang—"I'd be willing to wager a whole quarter's pay that they're making that kind of aerial bombs at the munitions plant. Makes sense. They're going to great lengths to keep its location secret. Why construct an armaments factory so far away from military installations unless the armaments themselves are highly dangerous—and classified?"

Christopher's mouth flattened into a line. "Then we find that factory and wipe it from the earth."

"But it's the *how* of it I'm trying to determine." She pushed to her feet. Looking at the plans, she noted what must be ground gun installations. "If we positioned the *Demeter* right beside the munitions plant and simply unloaded all our guns into them, without a doubt their ground defense would shoot us down before we could do enough real damage."

"Our heavy guns are all ether powered."

"Still won't be enough. This," she said, pointing to the schematic, "is solid stone, doubtless several yards thick. We've already talked about it. They'd make it impervious to an airship's attack. The only way to take it down is from the inside. This is a state-of-the-art facility. Sabotage would be out of the question, so I know I'd have to bring my own explosives in."

He raised a brow. "Planting bombs was your strategy all along, before the *Demeter* came along."

"It was, but I'd hoped to take advantage of her strength to help me in my mission."

"*Our* mission," he said. "And with what were you intending to construct these bombs, had our paths not fortuitously crossed?"

She grinned. "I earned very high marks in my explosive-device training back at Greenwich. With a few key elements, most of which I can scrounge or concoct, I can build a bomb that would turn the Black Forest into the Black Matchsticks."

He rolled his eyes. "Only you would boast about your bomb-making skills."

"Remember that time I tried to cook? *Tournedos Mirabeau*. Nearly burned your lodgings down."

"And yourself. Your skirts caught on fire."

"Which you tore off and threw out the window. Scared the bobby outside half to death."

It was not her most dignified moment, in a life frequently characterized by a shortage of dignity. "I may not be able to cook a meal," she continued, "but I *can* cook explosive devices."

He looked thoughtful, then strode to the door and opened it. "Follow me."

"Where are we going?"

"You're in espionage, so I suppose it can't be helped that you aren't very trusting. In this instance, though, you're going to have to be."

Back through the ship's passages they went. She mentally reviewed the schematics of the *Demeter*, trying to ascertain their destination. Admittedly, when she'd looked at the plans, she'd been concerning herself more with all the places on the ship Christopher would visit frequently. But she didn't recognize the passageway down which he now led her.

He stopped before a door, then nodded toward it. "Go on. Open it."

"There isn't a famished tiger behind this door, is there?"

"His roaring at night is so tedious. Now, open it."

She did so. And clapped her hands together like a girl stepping into a toyshop.

It was a long chamber, almost the length of the ship, and lined with racks. Within the racks were cannon shells.

Christopher grinned. "Welcome to your kitchen."

Chapter Six

DANGER LAY AS close as the nearby mountains, looming and gray. Christopher couldn't be at rest, not so long as his ship and crew were imperiled. Louisa was on his ship, too. It was his responsibility to keep her protected. Even had they been far from any ship, so long as she was near, he had to ensure her safety.

His duties kept him occupied all day. The repairing of an airship wasn't an easy matter, and though his crew and the master carpenter had been well-trained, he found himself called upon continually to make decisions and direct operations. He remained on his feet throughout the day and even took his midday meal standing up.

Despite the fullness of his hours, he continually found himself walking down the passageway that led to the magazine.

He stepped inside and watched Louisa as she worked. "Is the soup ready yet?"

He stepped into the chamber and surveyed her workspace. Someone had procured her a table, now covered with a waxed canvas cloth, and here she sat. A series of mirrors and prisms had been set up to bring the sunlight into the magazine, illuminating innumerable parts spread out upon the table. Wires, disassembled shells, and clockwork gears formed a chaotic mass that he couldn't decipher. It had to make sense to Louisa, for she bent over this jumble with a frown of concentration.

"You'd better take tea," she muttered without looking up. "It's going to be a while."

Reflected light flared over the lenses of her spectacles as she tightened the nut around a bolt joining two pieces of metal. More tools were arrayed beside her, including what looked like a watchmaker's screwdriver and pliers, a soldering iron, and a ebony-handled straight razor.

He picked up the razor and examined the handle. *To CR, Stay sharp, Love, LS.*

"This is mine." He kept it and the rest of his toiletries in a locked cabinet.

She did glance up then, briefly. "I thought it would be impolite if I asked one of the crew for their razors."

"But theft from me isn't impolite."

"Requisitioning, not stealing." Showing no remorse, she returned to her work, her hands busy with minute pins and screws. She'd taken the mass of her hair and fastened it up to keep it out of the way, but her efforts had been hasty, and several loose tendrils curled around her face and down the smooth line of her neck.

The urge to run the tips of his fingers along that silken curve made him knot his hands into fists.

"Tell me how I can help," he said. "More shells. Other materials from the ship."

"A cup of tea would set my heart aflutter."

He scowled. "Perhaps you didn't see the bars on my sleeve." He held them up. "Three of them."

"You asked."

"I'll send a boy down to wait on you." Annoyed at how quickly he rose to the bait, he headed toward the door.

"Don't need waiting on," she called after him. "Just a cup of tea. Extra sweet."

He was already out in the passageway, so she couldn't hear his muttered, "I remember." He used to tease her that she wouldn't have a single nub of a tooth left, the way she drank her sugary tea.

Allow me this much, she'd retort. *It's my one vice.*

Your most innocuous vice, he would answer.

I'll show you vice. And then she'd done just that.

He shook his head, trying to clear his thoughts. But it was no good. No matter where he was on the ship, no matter how entrenched in his duties, her presence haunted him. All he had to do was walk fifty yards, and he could see her again.

His anger at her past desertion kept slipping from his grasp, and their recent conversations only proved that he still loved talking with her, the dance and play of their words. Enjoying her company felt like self-betrayal, leading himself through a treacherous, stormy sky.

Returning topside, he continued to supervise the repairs, answering a hundred questions an hour. The smell of wood and metal hung over the ship, familiar. He drew it deep into his lungs. And yet he caught the faint scent of jasmine—her favorite fragrance. He dismissed the idea. There were several decks that lay between them, and even with his heightened senses, it would be ridiculous to think he could catch her scent all the way up there. Besides, she'd been on a covert mission. Unlikely that she'd periodically doused herself with toilet water.

Still, she formed a bright phantom at the back of his mind, impossible to ignore.

When afternoon light stretched shadows across the deck, he ventured back below. Back to the magazine, and her.

He found her standing with her back to the door, hands on her hips. She faced the table. On it sat an assembled mass of wires, tubes, brass, and wood. The object nearly covered the entire table. The bomb.

"That's not the posture of a woman reveling in her success."

She glanced over her shoulder at his approach, then back at her handiwork. "I haven't armed it yet, but don't break out the celebratory rum anytime soon."

"It's finished, isn't it? Your work is complete. Though it'll be damned tough to sneak something that big into the munitions plant."

"I can't make it any smaller. Not if I want it to have enough force to damage the internal structures of the factory."

He edged her aside and picked up the bomb easily. "I can carry it."

She stared at him for a moment, and he remembered

that she hadn't truly seen a demonstration of his Man O' War strength. Lightly, he set the explosive device back down onto the table.

"The ship will need her captain during the operation. You'll be wanted up here, not on the ground."

"Mr. Pullman is prepared to captain the ship if I'm needed elsewhere."

"And you're willing to play stevedore?"

"Whatever the operation necessitates." He raised an eyebrow. "Trying to scuttle the mission?"

"We may have to." She shook her head. "Bad news, Captain."

"Tell me."

"We need *three* of these bombs to destroy the munitions plant."

He cursed. "Even my strongest crewmen couldn't lift those things. Certainly not far enough."

Swearing, she kicked the leg of the table. "I went over my calculations four times. Everything in this bomb is exactly as it's supposed to be. There's no room for adjustment." She swore again, elaborately, and he recalled that she'd spent years around sailors, with the language to prove it.

"Can't be done." Pulling off her spectacles, she tossed them angrily beside her tools. "We're up to our arses in Hapsburgs and have a real chance to strike a blow against them, but it doesn't bloody matter because the sodding bombs are too sodding big."

"Hold." He faced her, cupping her elbows with his palms.

Hectic pink stained her cheeks, and her jaw clenched tight. Her hazel eyes glinted with anger—at herself. She'd always been toughest on herself, allowing others far more latitude and giving herself none.

"We know the answer's here somewhere," he continued. "It's just a matter of reasoning it out."

"I'm not fond of being patronized," she ground out.

"When in the whole of the time that we've known each other have I fed you palliative words? Don't insult me like that."

She muttered an apology.

"I'm telling you the truth," he said. "You earned top marks in constructing explosive devices, fine, but you did so in controlled conditions. Now's the time to show us all what you're made of. In that devious brain of yours lies the answer to this conundrum. It's there. Stop gnashing your teeth and pulling your hair, and find it."

At first, it appeared as though she'd turn some of her vitriol on him, but then she drew in a ragged breath, visibly fighting for calm.

"All right," she said. "All right." She glanced up. "No wonder you're so adept at leading your crew. Look how well you managed me."

They both realized at the same time that he still held her. He dropped his hands. Too late. Her warmth and feel had already imprinted upon his palms.

"The first thing I'll need . . . ."

"Tell me."

". . . is whiskey." Her eyes twinkled.

"And not for the bomb."

"For the bomb-maker." God, her smile could lay him out on the floor, bleeding and happy.

Deciding it would be more expeditious to simply fetch the whiskey himself rather than pulling one of the crew off of their duties, he gave her a mock salute and quickly left the magazine. Moments later, he returned with a bottle taken from his private reserve.

"A thousand blessings upon you." She uncorked the bottle and put it to her lips. Tilting her head back, she took a healthy swallow. "You can join me if you like."

"Very generous of you, considering it's my whiskey." But he took the bottle from her and drank. The burn pleasantly scalded its way down his throat.

For several minutes, they leaned against the table, passing the bottle back and forth. Surprising how companionable the quiet was between them, how easily they shared, like old friends.

The realization struck him. They had been more than lovers; they'd been friends. Beyond the time they spent in bed, he liked her, liked spending time with her. And when she'd walked out on him, she'd torn a hole in his life, her absence all the harder to bear because of that lost friendship.

He shook his head, then took another drink. Life could be a regular son of a bitch.

"Ah!" She slapped her palm against the table and shoved away it. "The explosive!" Facing him, she continued. "The bomb's size comes from the amount of explosive required. If I can find a way to concentrate it, make it more potent, I can drastically reduce the size of the device."

"Making it easier to transport and sneak into the munitions plant."

"Precisely." Excitement brightened her eyes and flushed her cheeks, and she looked so damned beautiful it was a sweet pain.

He set the bottle down and stood. "Chemistry's not my strength. Give me something that sails or flies, and I'm a wealth of information, but I wouldn't know the first thing about concentrating an explosive."

"Lucky, then, that I happen to be very good at it." She paced around the magazine, tapping her chin with her finger, deep in thought. "What's on this ship that can be used to supercharge an explosive? What can I combine with trinitrotoluene to make it more than double its power?"

In this, he was at a loss. He knew the best places at which to aim a cannon to create maximum damage. He could read the color and texture of the sky like a scholar pouring over tomes. He could tell from just a glance which of his crew would prove to be the strongest and most reliable. But the arcane world of chemistry left him directionless.

Ironic, given that his whole existence had been changed by scientific advancement. But you didn't wonder what made your heart beat. It simply did.

All he could do was watch Louisa as she paced and ruminated and muttered to herself. To watch the complex machinations of her mind, the play of thought across her face—it was unexpectedly fascinating. And arousing.

Suddenly, she stopped in her pacing. Her eyes went wide as she looked him. "Telumium."

"What of it?"

"I read some intercepted communications between Swedish scientists. They were discussing a new use for telumium. When combined with an explosive, such as trinitrotoluene—"

"TNT."

She nodded. "When combined with TNT in different proportions, the telumium infused the explosive with tremendous power. They've been experimenting with it to use in mining, but it might also work with a bomb. I can conduct some experiments of my own. What I need," she said with a concerned press of her mouth, "is a source of telumium."

"The *Demeter* happens to have a telumium source." He glanced at his left shoulder, then at her. "Me."

LOUISA STARED AT Christopher. "Are you sure? The gathering panels mounted in the ship's bulkheads also contain telumium."

"They're alloys. What's been grafted to my skin is the pure form of the metal. It's what you'll need for your experiments." Confidence deepened his already sonorous voice.

He was right. The Swedish scientists alluded to using unadulterated telumium, and if she added in unknown elements, the results would be either ineffective or possibly disastrous. Before she could even open her mouth to agree, however, he'd already taken off his coat and was undoing the buttons of his waistcoat.

She couldn't take her gaze from the sight of his long, broad-tipped fingers slipping the buttons through their holes. "Ah, um, very good." She cleared her suddenly dry throat. "You'll need to, ah, expose the implants so I can take a sample."

His only response was a slight tilt in the corner of his mouth. Shrugging out of his waistcoat, his shirt clung adoringly to his shoulders and arms, the material fine enough to hint at the skin beneath. He unknotted then whipped off his neck cloth. It dropped to the growing pile of clothing on the floor. He tugged his shirttails out of his breeches and worked at the buttons, starting at the top.

Slowly, his flesh was revealed. His neck. The hollow at the base of his throat. The span between his pectorals, lightly brushed with red-gold hair. The top of his ridged abdomen, then lower, to the indentation of his navel, and below, where a thin trail of more hair traced down his flat stomach to vanish beneath the waistband of his breeches.

He peeled away the shirt and added it to his discarded clothes. She was conscious of his gaze on her, conscious that he could see every play of emotion and need, but for all her skill at deception, she couldn't hide her reaction to him.

"Oh," she breathed, "what a wonder is science."

She'd known that he had physically changed as a result of the implants, had seen hints and glimpses, but here he was, nude from the waist up, and the transformation was astonishing.

Where once he'd been lean and compactly muscled, now he possessed the exaggerated masculine beauty of a summer god. The delineations of his abdominal muscles were precise, his chest broad, his arms potently hewn. Her gaze strayed farther up to his shoulders, wide as the sky itself. Her searching perusal stopped when she finally beheld the telumium implants.

Metal had been fused to the skin of his left shoulder and pectoral, sculpted in the shape of muscle, like Roman armor. The telumium gleamed in the reflected sunlight, and her fingers itched to touch it.

She actually took a step forward, hand upraised, before realizing what she was doing.

"Touch it," he murmured. "You won't hurt me."

Closing the distance between them, she stood very close and saw herself reflected in the telumium. Her breath misted slightly on the implants. She brought her hand up slowly, tentatively, before lightly touching her fingertips to the metal.

"Warm."

"It heats me, and I heat it." He raised his arm smoothly. "One of the unique properties of telumium. It retains its strength and durability but is also flexible, so no mobility is lost."

She bent even closer, studying the metal. This was the first time she'd ever seen actual Man O' War implants. There had been photos and cinemagraphs, but never had she beheld this with her own eyes, felt its heat and strange suppleness beneath her fingers.

He'd said the procedure had taken many painful hours. Seeing the seamless way in which the telumium was integrated with his flesh, she could believe it. He must have wanted this very badly to have endured so much. She'd been trained in resisting torture, but she doubted she could have borne what he had.

Glancing up, she saw him watching her guardedly. Tension tightened along his jaw and neck.

He was troubled. By what she might think of him. Of this final proof that he had truly altered into something not entirely human.

"It's beautiful," she whispered.

Heat flared in his gaze before he looked away.

She wanted to touch the rest of him, too. Not merely to test the new strength of his body, but to feel *him*, this man she had known and cared for. His unique combination of bravado and kindness that challenged and cherished her. The gleam of purpose as well as humor in his gaze. When she pushed, he pushed back, and when she needed tenderness, his arms had always been ready to hold her close.

The drumming of her pulse revealed that she cared for him still. Wanted him. He might desire her, but what of his heart? Could she move past her own fear?

She had to keep silent. They had reached a tentative entente, perhaps even a small fragment of friendship, and if she spoke of her heart, she could destroy it all. He had every right to push her away. She must give him no cause to.

Pulling back, she tried to speak briskly. "If you'll just sit there," she nodded toward the chair, "I'll take some samples."

He moved fluidly to take a seat. Without his shirt, in

motion, his body was a brutal poem. She attempted to steady herself by grabbing her spectacles and meticulously polishing them with a small cloth. After donning her glasses, she sorted through her tools to find precisely what she needed. She selected a rasp and a smaller file, then pulled out another chair to sit beside him.

Despite the fact that they had been in the magazine together for some time, the chamber felt a good deal smaller now. He seemed to fill the space with his presence. Lacking the barrier of his clothing, he exuded heat, and her own skin warmed to be so close to him. He stared straight ahead, hands braced on his knees, as Louisa bent close to the implants.

"Let me know at any time if you feel the slightest discomfort."

He gave a slight nod.

With a piece of paper cupped just beneath to collect the filings, she began to run the rasp along the metal. The angle was awkward, her purchase minimal, as she was trying not to touch his bare flesh. The rasp skidded over the telumium, succeeded only in creating a few scrapes. A tiny flake of metal drifted down onto the paper. At this rate, by the time she gathered enough telumium, the Hapsburgs would conquer London.

"Could you hold this here?" She pressed the paper into his right hand and guided it to the proper position beneath his implant.

Drawing a breath, she cupped her free hand around his bicep to hold it steady as she worked.

They both hissed in a breath at the sensation.

Good god, it was as if his whole body was made of metal. He'd never been a loose and flabby man, far from it, but now he was impossibly hard and solid. She could hardly believe she touched flesh, save for the slight yield to the pressure of her fingers and the hot, satiny feel of his skin. Yet more than these changes, she was acutely aware that it was *Christopher* she touched. And she touched a place reserved for intimacy. How many nights had she gripped him, just here, as he stretched above her, with her legs wrapped around his waist and the dimmed gaslight all around them like antique gold? How often had she watched the bunch and flex of muscles in his arms as he gripped the headboard, her atop him, riding them both toward ecstasy?

Desire and sorrow combined within her in a mystifying alchemy, so she could not separate one from the other.

Mouth pressed tight, she made herself focus on her work. She ran the rasp back and forth across the implant. With the additional leverage, she had more success, and curls of metal gathered on the paper.

"This doesn't hurt?"

"No."

"Even if it did, you wouldn't tell me, would you?"

"No."

She scanned his face for any signs that he might be in pain, but there was no way to know if the lines bracketing his mouth came from her scraping at his implants, or him simply having to endure her touch. Unless he said otherwise, she'd just have to proceed.

The only sounds in the magazine came from the rasp and the faint noise of repairs continuing throughout the ship. Someone in the passageway outside walked by, whistling an old sea shanty.

She thought being this close to Christopher might help her get used to him, that she could hold his arm and feel its weight, and think of him as any man. Take away some of the mystique. The opposite proved to be true. For the more she touched him and saw up close the rise and fall of his chest—the same chest on which she used to rest her head—the more she ached and wanted and cursed herself.

The tension within the magazine ratcheted higher, far more explosive than the powder in the cannon shells.

She could stand it no longer.

"I could never become anyone's wife, Christopher," she said quietly. "I made no secret of it. But you asked me, anyway."

He tensed, as if her words had been an unexpected blow. For several moments, he didn't speak. Perhaps he'd simply ignore her. She couldn't decide whether to press him, or just continue with her work.

Then, "It's what men typically do," he said tightly, his face in pristine profile, "when they fall in love."

"We aren't typical, you and I."

"True. Typical women don't react to a marriage proposal by running off on a mission without leaving even a damned note." He kept his body still, but he stared at her. "D'you know, I didn't find out where you'd gone until Admiral Davidson told me at a briefing. That you were overseas for an indefinite period of time. Apparently, you'd begged him for the assignment and left that very day."

Her gaze dropped away. "That wasn't . . . well done of me."

He snorted.

"But, Christopher," she said, spreading her hands, "I didn't know what to do when you asked."

"If you didn't want to marry me, you could have said no. Better that than running."

"I know you, Christopher. If someone says no, you redouble your efforts. You don't stop until you get exactly what you want. I'm just as stubborn." She struggled to find the words, fumbling through the chaos of her own emotions. "We would've battered against each other until we were nothing but dust."

"There's such a thing as compromise."

Her brows rose. "Since when has either of us compromised?"

"You didn't even goddamn *try*."

"It's true. I was . . . a coward." She stared down at the tools now resting in her lap. So simple, so elegant, these tools. If she faced a mechanical problem, it was a matter of working the situation out, slowly, thoroughly, until a solution was found. "A coward in many ways. I was . . . afraid. To say no to your face. Afraid you'd change my mind. Afraid that if you did, we'd just . . . make each other miserable."

Fear gripped her now. Could she ever make things right between them? They could never go back to what they had before, but they couldn't go on this way. Neither friends nor enemies. A volatile mixture of both.

He set the paper with the filings on the table before swinging around to face her. "I was so goddamn happy being with you. And you were happy being with me. Where in any of that did you see a future of misery?"

"Marriage changes people, changes how they see each other, treat each other." Restless, she put her tools and spectacles aside, and walked tight circles around the perimeter of the magazine. How to articulate her feelings to him when she didn't fully understand them herself?

"I've seen it so many times," she continued. "The courtship and the first years after a wedding—everything's wonderful. The love between the couple is a palpable thing, hot and alive and shining. But then . . ." Words and fears smashed against each other. A struggle to break free, to verbalize what she only now could fully comprehend. " . . . that love changes. Withers. Or dies altogether."

He shot to his feet. "It doesn't have to. Yes, maybe it does change, but not into something worse. Into . . . something different." Like her, he wrestled with words. "Something perhaps even better than that consuming fire. There's trust . . . and comfort. And strength."

"What of passion? You say that trust, comfort, and strength are better, but I couldn't live without passion."

"Did we ever lack passion?" He stalked close. "Could something so bright fade?"

He wrapped one iron-hard arm around her waist, and brought his other hand up to cup the back of her head. His gaze raked her for a moment, eyes bright as blue fire.

They had both exhausted the limitations of words. Action was far more articulate.

His mouth came down onto hers.

At the first touch of his lips to hers, need tore through her. She clung to his shoulders, one of flesh, one of metal, yet she felt all of him at once. The long, unyielding length of his body. His large hands holding her tightly. The sensation of his mouth, hot and demanding. She knew him, his mouth, had tasted countless of his kisses, but he was different now. Taller. Tougher. Angrier.

There was a consuming hunger as he kissed her, as his tongue swept into her mouth. Yet she wasn't cowed into submission. She met his kiss with her own demand. It had been so long. Since she'd shared this with him. Since she had burned from the inside out. She gripped him, hard, pressing herself against him.

He tasted of whiskey, tobacco, and regret for what could have been.

She wasn't aware of being walked backwards until the racks of shells rattled against her back. At the sound, he abruptly released her and stepped away. Her hands hovered in the air for a moment before she slowly lowered them.

Now the only sound in the magazine came from them as they panted, fighting for breath and sense. Her breathing slowed, but sense didn't return. She was alight with desire. Her yearning body knew him, wanted him, and so did her heart.

His face was dark, either from anger or arousal or both. The great mass of his body shuddered.

She said, "I have to—"

He held up a hand, silencing her. "Don't."

But she wouldn't be silenced. "I have to apologize. I'm sorry, Christopher. So sorry."

"I'm not sorry I kissed you." His eyes seemed to glow.

"I'm not either." She, who never cried, blinked back tears. "But I am sorry about what I did three years ago. I made a mistake. I ran, when I shouldn't have. I didn't give us a chance. Now . . . I don't know what to do."

He smiled mirthlessly. "I've flown this ship through storms that had our compasses spinning. Captained a sea ship that was blown thousands of miles off course by a hurricane. But I've never been as lost as I am in this room." He eyed the distance between them. "In this, we're both adrift."

Chapter Seven

CHRISTOPHER STAYED CLOSE. The heat of their kiss kept him in Louisa's orbit. If questioned—which he wouldn't be—he had a convenient reason to remain near. There was no way to know how much telumium she would need for the bombs, compelling him to remain with her in the magazine as she conducted her experiments. She tried various amounts of the metal, making small adjustments as necessary, and taking more filings from his implant.

In truth, he might have insisted she take a larger amount of telumium at once, thus enabling him to leave the magazine and find work elsewhere in the ship. God knew he had enough to do. Yet he remained with her as the afternoon edged toward early evening. Every five minutes, someone in his crew popped his head in and asked him different questions. If the crewmen thought it strange that the ship's captain sat shirtless in the magazine with a woman from Naval Intelligence, they wisely kept their mouths shut. Around him, anyway.

He watched her work, fascinated by the process that only she seemed to understand. Her hands were nimble, precise, and a small line appeared between her brows as she concentrated. She'd always frowned when working out a puzzle. In the few years since they'd been apart, the line had grown a little deeper, become more permanent. Tiny lines fanned out in the very corners of her eyes. She hadn't needed the spectacles three years ago, either.

She was a woman. A woman who subtly aged with the passage of time. Who made mistakes, and admitted to them.

He didn't know if it made it worse or better that she'd done so. A few words couldn't undo the damage she'd caused. Yet the fact that she had understanding and courage enough to own up to her actions helped solder shut the giant fractures in his heart.

One thing he *wasn't* comforted by: the knowledge that she desired him still. He'd tasted it in her kiss. Felt it in the grip of her hands on him, how her body molded to his. His own body still tightened in readiness. His appetite had been whetted. But it was a hunger that had to go unsatisfied. This was not the time. Not the place.

He might go to his death wanting her.

To occupy himself in between her taking more telumium, he picked up and studied whichever tool she wasn't using. Turned them over and over in his hands and felt their wooden handles, their metal pieces.

"A wondrous age of mechanical marvels, this is," he murmured. "When I was a boy, no one had heard of *aurorae vires*, nor telumium. Ether, too, was just a subject of speculation."

Still bent over her work, she added, "Tetrol was only a rumor, also. Wild stories told by visitors to China. Vast soya bean fields being turned into fuel that burned faster and cleaner than coal. Who'd have believed it?"

"Now all of it's real." He spun a screwdriver on the tip of his finger. "My very existence proves it."

Reaching over, she snatched the screwdriver away with a single, deft move, and used it to make adjustments on the bomb. "Wonder what the next few decades will bring."

"Something marvelous, or terrible."

"Or both."

"Can something be both marvelous and terrible?"

She gazed at him. "Love."

He made a soft snort of agreement. "Perhaps we should send a telegram to Dr. Rossini. Suggest she study the scientific properties of love. She could power half of London's electricity if she found a way to harness love's energy."

"It wouldn't be a very reliable power source." She turned to him and ran the rasp over his implant, one hand on his arm. It didn't matter that she'd touched him thusly half a dozen times in the past few hours. One brush of her fingertips against his bare skin and his pulse raced like a turbine.

"Maybe not." He stared down at the crown of her head, where the lamplight turned her hair to gleaming mahogany. "But there are always new fools falling in love."

After a few passes of the rasp, she hunched over the worktable again. "We'll have to find another scientist to conduct the experiments. Dr. Rossini is a bloody hard woman to find."

"I heard her flying city was last seen over the coast of West Africa."

"And I heard she'd been spotted over Brazil," he said. "She and that group of rogue Man O' Wars that believe her some kind of god, or queen, or both. She doesn't disabuse them of the notion, or so I've heard. The *Hera* had a run in with that flying city of hers. The ship was almost shot from the sky."

"The price of genius is often madness. Me, I'd rather have just enough brilliance to keep everyone in awe of me, but not so much that it chips away at my sanity. And I do think that this qualifies as a work of brilliance." She straightened, pushing her hair out of her face, and gestured to the device on the table.

"This can't be a big enough bomb." It was a metal box nearly the same size as a cannon shell for one of his four-inch guns, covered by a lace of wires and tubes. A clock face had been welded to one side of the box, with wires connecting it to the device. "Looks too damned small."

"Never underestimate the small things." She stood and stretched, bracing her hands against the small of her back and arching. A series of small pops traveled up the length of her spine. She sighed, and when she caught him staring at her outthrust breasts, she chuckled.

"Are you ready?" she asked, her voice a husky murmur.

He dragged his gaze up to her face. His brain had slowed to a cruising speed. "For what?"

She patted the bomb. "Let's put this chemistry of ours to the test."

Crewmen gathered at the starboard rail of the ship. Those that couldn't make it topside pressed against the starboard portholes. Still, there wasn't room enough for everyone, and so news was being relayed from man to man as new developments occurred. Right now, they were silent as Louisa made final adjustments to her bomb.

Those who could see what she was doing whispered to one another. Christopher didn't need his heightened hearing to catch what the crew said.

"Ain't possible for that puny thing to do no decent damage on a ground target."

"What's she going to blow up with it? A dollhouse?"

Christopher kept his concerns to himself. By the hard set of her mouth, he could tell Louisa felt the pressure of hope and expectation. Everyone needed the bomb to work, for the sake of the mission. Adding his voice to the chorus of doubt served no purpose. He merely watched and offered his silent support.

Turning to Pullman, he asked, "The ship's in proper working order?"

"Aye, sir." The first mate's gaze moved over the deck, assessing. "Told the men we needed the repairs done on the double. They're raising the anchor, too."

He glanced toward where a crewman turned on a tetrol-powered crane to hoist anchor. The machine started with a high whine, and heat rippled out from the engine's exhaust pipe. Steadily, the anchor went up.

"Give the crew my commendation, Mr. Pullman. And an extra ration of rum with dinner."

"Aye, sir!"

Testing the bomb had several risks. The bomb itself could fail, or be unstable. It could detonate at the wrong time. And if it did explode, the concussion would give away the *Demeter*'s position to any Hapsburg ships possibly nearby. If they attracted the attention of the enemy, they'd need to make a fast escape, or else be prepared for a battle.

Christopher didn't like the prospect of fleeing, but he needed his ship at her fullest capability and strength. A skirmish with an enemy airship was simply too risky.

He waited, hands clasped behind his back, as Louisa completed her adjustments. At last, she straightened, holding the bomb in her arms.

"We're ready," she said.

At Christopher's nod, the master at arms shouted, "Make way!"

Crewmen stepped back, forming a path for her as she approached the starboard rail. She'd chosen the starboard side rather than port side because the mountains were tallest on the starboard, and could absorb the sound better.

She balanced it on the rail, then adjusted the dial on the clock. Christopher saw now that it was a timer, and she had set it for fifteen seconds.

"On my count," Louisa said.

Everyone, Christopher included, held their breath. He, too, waited at the rail.

"Three, two, one. Now!"

She dropped the bomb over the side and immediately pulled out a stopwatch.

The bomb fell, fell. Crewmen with spyglasses followed the downward progress of the bomb. Christopher didn't need a spyglass and did not lose sight of the small object as it grew even smaller in its descent.

Louisa glanced at her stopwatch, then shouted, "Brace yourselves!"

The bomb exploded.

No one, not even Christopher, expected the size of the blast. It billowed out in a huge, fiery sphere. Astonished swears and shouts rose up from the crew as the airship rocked from the force of the explosion. Had the bomb been on the deck of the ship when it had detonated, the mountains would be littered with the crew and pieces of the *Demeter*.

Silence followed. And then cheers from the crew.

A throng formed around her as men pushed in to shake her hand. Smiling, she accepted their acclaim with bright-eyed satisfaction.

One bold soul, a very young midshipman, moved to kiss her cheek. He took one look at Christopher and settled for a handshake before scurrying away.

"Alright, men," Christopher shouted above the din, "let's not linger and give the Huns something to shoot at."

A chorus of "Aye, Cap'n" followed before the crew dispersed. As men hastened to their stations, Christopher stepped close to Louisa. She stared up at him as he bent down and brushed a kiss on her cheek.

"Well done, Lulu," he murmured.

The pleasure in her gaze burned brighter, and her

already wind-pinkened skin turned a deeper rosy hue. "Couldn't have done it without you, Kit."

Men shouted to one another as the ship made ready to fly. The *Demeter* gave a single, hard shudder when the turbine roared to life. By slow degrees, the ship moved forward, gaining speed as she flew. Mountains unrolled below, including the site of the explosives test.

At Christopher's direction, the ship was guided up and over the mountain. Once on the other side, it sank lower, using the mountain for concealment.

And none too soon. Just before the *Demeter* dipped into the shadows, Christopher spotted the prow of a ship. He recognized the gryphon figurehead. It belonged to the Hapsburg ship *Kühnheit*. And it headed in their direction.

"The enemy," he muttered. "Investigating the explosion, no doubt."

Louisa glanced at him, only the slightest tension in her shoulders betraying her unease.

The *Demeter* slipped lower over the mountain. He lost sight of the Hapsburg ship.

He turned to the helmsman. "Keep her steady and low. Let's pray the Huns haven't seen us. We need to play the shy maiden for a while."

"Stay hidden, sir," answered Dawes. "Aye, sir."

The order to remain silent was quietly given to the crew over the shipboard auditory device. Stillness fell heavily, a marked contrast to the cheers from earlier.

Christopher stayed at the rail, Louisa beside him, as

the ship skimmed along the side of the mountains. With the rocky peaks forming a barrier, there was no way to know if the enemy spotted them. He kept his hearing attuned to the sound of an approaching airship—difficult to do with the *Demeter*'s own engines growling and the whistle of the wind. The warning might come too late.

For several tense minutes, the ship flew on, trying to put as much distance as possible between her and the site of the bomb test.

Only after half an hour had passed with no sounds of pursuit did Christopher relax. "Resume normal duties," he instructed over the audio.

The ship seemed to sigh with relief.

"You'd need a Sheffield razor for a closer shave," Louisa murmured.

He smiled slightly, and though he had to maintain vigilance, she helped unhook the gaffs of edgy restlessness dug into his heart. "Had a Sheffield razor, given to me by a pretty woman. A shame that a wily, bomb-making spy stole it from me."

"Requisitioned it," she corrected.

"Tell yourself whatever fictions you need, but we both know you've got sticky fingers."

"Sticky as treacle."

Late afternoon light gilded the deck of the ship. It caught in Louisa's tumbling curls and along the curve of her cheek, sweeping over the straight lines of her shoulders. A few high clouds seemed to catch fire, spreading wisps of flame across the sky.

Louisa on the top deck of his airship as the day reached

its burning conclusion: Many times over the years, he'd tormented himself with this very image. It had been everything he'd ever wanted, and everything he had abjured. Now, with the ship far behind enemy lines, she was truly there. Reality was far more complex than any of his imaginings.

LOUISA HAD ONLY dined at the captain's table once—the day before. Yet her absence felt like half the lamps in the room had been extinguished.

"Is Miss Shaw not joining us, sir?" asked Lieutenant Brown. Disappointment was writ plainly on his face.

Christopher stared at the place that had been set for her, wishing she was there, as well. "She's the only person on this ship who can build the three bombs we need. The task may take her all night."

"If she had an assistant or two, sir, the work might go faster."

"Already been offered, Lieutenant. She told me, and I quote, 'I have neither the time nor the patience to school a bunch of ham-fisted sailors on the delicate, dangerous work of timed explosives.' When I was more insistent that she have help in her work, Miss Shaw told me that the *Demeter* was my ship, and if I wanted to blow her up, that was my decision."

"A woman confident in her skills," Pullman said with a smile.

"After this afternoon, no one can doubt her." Christopher waved the steward over. "Has Miss Shaw eaten?"

"Mr. Duffy sent Fitzroy down with a tray to the magazine, sir," Vale answered. "The boy said she took a bite or two. Had her head down most of the time, and told Fitzroy to leave the tray. I can check to see if she's eaten more."

"I'll do it." Christopher rose from the table. He waved the men back down when they moved to stand.

"Very conscientious, sir." Dr. Singh smiled over the rim of his wine glass. "Seeing after Miss Shaw's health. I may lose my post."

The other officers chuckled.

"And I may have you thrown in the brig for insubordination, Doctor." But Christopher grinned as he said this, and he strode from the officers' mess.

En route to the magazine, he stopped in to talk with the navigator. "Miss Shaw gave you the coordinates?"

"Aye, sir. She felt that this chain here"—Herbert pointed to a line of mountains on the chart spread in front of him— "would be the most likely spot for the weapons plant, and that's where we're headed. But it's a big chain, sir, and isolating the one mountain is going to prove a challenge."

"We'll navigate that channel when we come to it. Good night, Mr. Herbert."

" 'Night, sir."

He found Louisa just as he expected: hunched over the table, meticulously assembling small pieces of metal. Night had fallen, so the pale green glow of quartz lamps provided illumination as she worked. Open flames from gas lamps posed too much of a danger to the massive amounts of gunpowder stored within the room.

"Come to check on your one-woman munitions plant, Christopher?" she asked without looking up.

"How'd you know it was me and not someone else in the crew?"

"No one else on the ship walks as you do. There's more weight and purpose in your tread. As though you're needed somewhere. Which, I imagine, you are." She offered a shrug, still immersed in her work. "Everyone's got a particular cadence to their stride. Listen close enough and you'll hear it. Mr. Tydings favors his right leg. An old wound, I'd wager. And your Master at Arms stomps around as if he were in a bad temper, but when he thinks no one's around, he walks lighter."

She missed nothing, his Louisa.

Strange that it didn't burn like acid to think of her that way.

"My own acute powers of observation detect that you've barely touched your meal." The tray of food sat on a crate, and he nudged it with his hand.

"No time to eat. If we reach the munitions plant tomorrow, the bombs need to be ready."

"And if you get too hungry, your energy will flag, your concentration will falter, and you might make a mistake." He grabbed the tray and carried it to her. "You have to eat something."

She finally looked up. The quartz light painted her face in unearthly radiance, yet fatigue ringed pale shadows beneath her eyes.

"An order, Captain?"

"A friendly request. One that I strongly suggest you follow." He held the tray toward her. When she opened her mouth to object, he added, "I'm not leaving this magazine until you've at least finished the soup and bread. Duffy was very proud of the soup."

She heaved a sigh but took the tray from him. With no room left on the table, she balanced the tray on her knees. He straddled the other chair, his arms braced across the back, and watched her.

She fixed him with an irritated look. "You really mean to nanny me through my supper?"

"It's your own stubbornness that impels me to do this. Now, eat."

"No wonder command comes so easily to you," she muttered. "Never met a man so convinced of his own primacy."

"And I've never met a woman so determined to work herself to exhaustion."

After giving him another scowl, she took a sip of soup. Her face brightened. "It's delicious. *Coulis de Volaille, dit à la Reine.*"

"Mr. Duffy would weep with joy that you know the name of his soup."

Between hasty spoonfuls, she said, "Part of my training. Disguises."

He remembered. She had to be able to blend in anywhere, under any circumstances, from the tables of the elite to the meanest taverns.

"I'd still be able to recognize you," he said, "no matter how you obscured yourself."

"None of my intended targets knows me as well as you do."

His gaze strayed to her mouth. He could never forget her taste, nor the feel of her lips against his. Desire roared to full wakefulness. To take her hair down and run his hands through the dark cascade. To nuzzle against the juncture of her neck and shoulders, inhale her warm, sweet fragrance. To feel the taut softness of her calves, her legs, and to take his hands higher . . .

"Don't." There was something almost desperate in her voice. "I can't . . . think about that now. I need all my wits, and you've a way of stealing them. Especially when you look at me like that."

He tore his gaze away. The effort not to touch her made his hands ache.

To distract himself, he studied the progress of her work. Two cannon shells sat on the table, as well as the components for assembling another bomb—a morass of wires, gears, and bits of metal. Telumium shavings glinted within an enameled cup.

"These are for harvesting more gunpowder." He tapped one of the cannon shells.

"That's actually one of the bombs. I'm housing them within empty shells. Unscrew the top, and you'll see."

He did so. Inside the shell was a complex network of wires surrounding a metal box, with another clock face surmounting the device. He raised his brows. "Ingenious."

A quick flare of gratification shone in her eyes before she suppressed it behind a façade of professional disinterest. "Makes them easier and more discreet to transport.

No one in the munitions plant will have cause to wonder why we're strolling about with cannon shells."

He replaced the top of the shell. "You've thought of everything. When it comes to using subterfuge, I haven't got your talent."

"A stand-up fight and full steam ahead." She smiled. "Explains why you're such a good ship's captain."

He shrugged off her praise. "I do what I'm supposed to."

"This isn't the first ship I've ever been on." She pointed at him with her spoon. "I've seen many captains in action. Some are good at commanding but have little concern for the men themselves. Ships run by fear or intimidation. Some captains are too anxious to be liked, and there's no discipline. Everything falls apart."

"Captain Gregg and Captain Villiers. Those were two captains I sailed with when I was a young seaman. Gregg was a right bastard. Caned and birched us boys at the slightest perceived offense. Still have a few scars."

"I've seen them," she said quietly.

Despite the unpleasant memories, heat coursed through him, remembering her hiss of sympathy the first time she'd seen the light web of scars on his back, and how she'd gently traced her fingers over the raised flesh. Her touch had turned sensuous, and they'd tangled together in the already knotted sheets.

He forced both recollections from his mind. "Villiers was a great one for telling a story or making the crew laugh, but when we found ourselves caught between the French and Brazilian navies, no one knew what to do, least of all him. If it hadn't been for the first mate, we wouldn't have made it out alive."

"There, you see? You *are* a good captain. Not everyone is able. You've just proven my point."

"And you haven't finished your soup."

"Though you're rather overbearing." She returned to her meal, however.

In short order, she not only ate her soup and bread, but the stewed venison, glazed carrots, and gooseberry fool, along with a glass of Burgundy.

She dabbed at her mouth with a linen napkin. "Hadn't realized how hungry I was."

"And now you're in the pink of health." The shadows beneath her eyes had lessened, and a bloom of color crested her cheeks. "You can't complain now about me being high handed."

"The only thing worse than the pronouncements of an overbearing man is proving him correct." Still, she gave him a quick smile. "Thank you. For . . ." Her gaze skittered away. ". . . taking care of me."

"My pleasure." And it was. Seeing the color return to her face and the ebbing of her fatigue filled him with a profound satisfaction. He couldn't pretend that he would feel the same about any guest who happened to be aboard his ship. No, it was her alone, tending to her needs, seeing her cared for, that gratified him.

You damned fool. It's happening all over again, and you can't stop it.

Needing distance, he stood. He plucked the tray from her lap and took several steps backward.

"Yes," she said with a nod, "I've another bomb to build."

"Anything on the ship is available to you."

Her gaze held his as they both realized the implications of his words. It was too bloody close to the truth. He moved to the door, but her voice stopped him.

"Kit." Softly spoken, barely more than a whisper. The sound of his name, reserved only for intimacy, was a heated caress.

He turned.

She glanced down at the tray in his hands. "It just occurred to me that if we reach the munitions plant tomorrow, that might have been my last dinner."

They both knew that his denials would ring hollow. Death had always been a possibility with this mission. He could only give a brief, terse nod.

"If that's true," she said quietly, her eyes dark and full, "then I'm glad it was spent with you."

He swallowed hard, throat tight. "Me, too." Wanting to toss the tray to the floor and sweep her into his arms, but knowing that they hadn't the time for any distractions, he forced himself to leave the magazine.

Life truly is a son of a bitch. The thought echoed again in his head as he strode down the passageway, away from her.

Chapter Eight

LOUISA'S EYES FLEW open. Disorientation swirled as she stared up at an unfamiliar wooden ceiling. She turned her head and saw not racks of cannon shells or her worktable, but a bookcase and a desk. No quartz lamps burned. The only illumination in the cabin came from the star-strewn sky outside the window, turning the interior faintly ash-colored, with the heavy pieces of furniture forming dark but not threatening shapes. She knew this chamber. Where was she?

She inhaled and caught the scent of hot metal and male flesh.

Christopher's quarters.

And she lay in Christopher's berth.

Dim recollections filtered through her memory. She had finished the very last bomb around two in the morning, but exhaustion had overwhelmed her before she could make the long journey back to Christopher's cabin, and bed. She had laid her head upon the table in the gunnery, promising herself that she'd just rest her eyes a moment, and then she'd get up and hie herself to bed. Clearly, her eyes had been closed longer than a moment. She must have fallen asleep.

But how did she get all the way from the magazine to the cabin?

Another image sieved through her mind. More remembered sensations than actual images. Iron-hard arms had enclosed her, lifting her as though she weighed less than ether. She'd been pressed against a warm, solid chest, and her arms had encircled someone's neck. Her head had rested against a wide, unyielding shoulder, yet it had felt so comfortable, so secure.

Perhaps she'd muttered something, an objection to being carried like an invalid, for a deep voice had rumbled, "Quiet, tyrannical woman."

Christopher, again. He'd carried her from the magazine to his cabin. And put her to bed.

Pushing herself upright, she glanced beneath the covers and felt a curious stab of disappointment that she was still clothed. Her boots had been removed, however, and stood neatly by the side of the bed. Her hair fell about her shoulders. He'd taken the pins out.

She wished she had been awake, or could recall seeing this powerful man tending to her so conscientiously. Almost tenderly. Even without remembering, she could picture it well. His big hands working at the laces of her boots, and picking out pins from her hair, one by one, to set them aside on a nearby nightstand. The pins themselves formed a tiny, glinting pile, like a miniature metallic haystack.

This whole ship was his, all of her firepower, all of her might, and yet he looked after Louisa with patience and care. By rights, he could have simply left her in the magazine. He should have. He should have been in his own berth instead of taking care of her. They'd reach the munitions plant soon. He needed all the rest he could get in preparation for the task ahead.

But no. He'd seen to her, instead.

She rose and began to undress. Her garments for the field were far more practical than what she wore when back at home. Nothing laced or fastened up the back. She had to be able to take everything on and off without assistance.

Rather like a whore, she thought with an inward smile.

Her parents didn't approve of her work. They had wanted her to join the family business translating legal documents. There was a clerk at the firm, Paul Lewis, whom she knew her parents favored for a possible husband. She could stay at home, translating liens from Hindi into English, with a baby perched on her knee and another en route. Or so her parents, and Paul, had wanted.

Though numerous other women worked for Naval Intelligence, her parents still thought it scandalous that she would involve herself in such a vocation. They would have approved of her more had she decided to become a journalist. She wasn't invited home at Christmas nor to celebrate the Mechanical 20th. To Mr. and Mrs. Shaw, she might as well be a whore.

As she pulled off her blouse and stepped out of her skirt, she decided the sacrifice was worth it. She loved her work and had no regrets.

Only one, she thought.

She tugged harder than necessary on the fastenings of her corset. Though she wore a short, lightly boned corset, she still exhaled in relief when it came away from her body.

Now wearing only her chemise and pantalets, she sat down on the bed. She moved her hands back and forth over the clean but plain blanket. Standard naval issue. Woven on giant looms by clockwork millworkers. It could not be more common. Yet because it was Christopher's blanket, and had covered him for countless nights, significance had been woven in with the wool.

She lay herself down, preparing to sleep, but a moment after her head hit the pillow, her eyes were wide open.

How could she sleep? Knowing that at some point during the next twenty-four hours, she might meet her death? She'd never feared it—every time she went out on assignment, there was always the possibility she might not come back. But that same regret continued to burn at the back of her mind, her heart.

Three years. They'd been apart three years, and all because she'd been afraid.

The thought made her heart pound. It seemed so foolish now, her flight. She had taken a chance at happiness and tossed it into the incinerator. Her only consolation—

and it was a paltry one—was that she'd believed at the time that she had acted in the right.

Would he have become a Man O' War had she not fled? Would their lives have taken very different paths?

She ground her fists into her eyes. An exercise in futility, these questions. They could never be answered. The only certainty lay ahead, in the form of a munitions plant dug into the side of a mountain. Between now and then was a blank. No, not a blank, but an unwritten page. The pen was poised in her hand. It was up to her as to how to fill that page.

Abruptly, she sat up again.

Three years. Three years without him. Oh, she'd been busy. Running from mission to mission. London to Stockholm to New Constantinople to Bucharest. Never a moment's rest. And she'd done good work. Important work. Thousands of civilians, sailors, and soldiers owed their lives to the intelligence she'd gathered. She had no misgivings about those years.

But they'd been empty. She had no one to come home to. No one to dream of. She'd often caught herself thinking, *Oh, Kit will laugh to hear this*, or, *Kit won't believe it when I tell him*. A trove of stories and anecdotes and images that he'd never hear.

How hollow she'd been after she left him. How she missed sharing with him. She hadn't truly realized it until these past few days, with his laughter and his strength so near.

"I love him," she said aloud. Again, with more volume, "I love him."

And the hell of it was, she always had.

She threw aside the blanket and stood.

She was done with fear. Though she did not believe in predestination, she'd been given a rare chance. Something, some force greater than human understanding had put her in that barn and Christopher's ship nearby. Perhaps it was fate. Perhaps it was electromagnetic frequencies. The cause didn't matter. The most important thing was for Christopher to learn how she felt about him.

This couldn't wait for the morning. The morning would be too late. Glancing around the cabin, she looked for a robe to throw over her chemise. Trained though the crew might be, the sight of a woman in her underclothes running through the ship might prove disruptive.

Her borrowed coat would have to suffice. She pulled it on and moved toward the door. Her steps slowed, then stopped. She didn't know where Christopher slept while she was in his quarters. Could she bang on doors up and down the ship, looking for him? She'd look like an asylum escapee. It didn't matter. She could always explain that it had to do with the mission.

She walked quickly to the door and threw it open.

Christopher stood in the passageway outside.

He wore his shirtsleeves, breeches, and boots. He wasn't a captain in his uniform, but a man. A man with hunger in his eyes.

Without taking his gaze from hers, he stepped inside. Shut the door behind him. They stood only inches apart. Shadows were thick in the cabin, yet she could see the rapid rise and fall of his chest, the flare of his nostrils.

Tremendous heat poured from his body, penetrating her heavy coat, soaking into her body.

For a moment, they simply stared at one another. Poised on the edge of a precipitous fall.

Then—they crashed together.

He cradled her head in his hands, angling her mouth to his, as she wrapped her arms around him. Their lips met in reckless desire. She tumbled into the kiss, its hot need, tasting him with both long familiarity and a sense of discovery.

For he was stronger now. Power radiated from him. She felt it in his thick, bunching muscles, in the press of his body to hers. The vast potential of him—barely contained.

She strained against him, wanting to feel more.

With a growl, he broke the kiss long enough to pull off her coat. Then she wore only her thin chemise and pantalets, and when she pressed close she gave a soft moan. The fine cotton of his shirt provided almost no barrier to the feel of him, hard and sinewy, and he possessed the heat of an engine. She arched into the thick length of his cock, snug against the front of his breeches. He growled again and took her mouth.

The world spun as he turned them around, and she found herself between two solid surfaces—Christopher and the door.

He leaned into her, enfolding her with his arms, his kiss. It was almost painful, the way he held her so tightly against the door and his body. The ferocity of his kiss left her breathless and shaking, damp with need. There was an animal hunger in him, a beast unleashed that both frightened and aroused her.

She must have made some small noise of distress, because her front was suddenly chilled as he tore himself away. Dazed, she could only lean against the door and watch him standing in the middle of the cabin. His breathing sounded like a freight train, rough and loud. Fists curled at his sides, he turned away.

"Kit," she whispered. "Come back."

"Want you too much." His voice was a low rasp. "Both the man and the Man O' War."

She took a step toward him.

"Don't," he flung over his shoulder. In the dimness of his quarters, his shirt gleamed, the braces he wore forming a Y across his back and emphasizing the triangular shape of his torso. "So close to . . . losing control."

"You won't hurt me." She took another step.

He still would not look at her. "You don't know that. *I* don't know that. If I did anything, if I caused you any pain . . ." He snarled. "*No.*"

"Because of the implants?"

"Them, and my own need for you."

"Has it always been like this, since the implants? When you . . ." She struggled to get the words out, hating the images they brought into her mind. "When you make love?"

"Wouldn't know." He turned to face her, his expression stark.

The truth struck her like a blow to her chest. "You haven't been with anyone else."

"Not since that November morning." His look turned dark. "Don't tell me if you have. I'd tear the ship apart if I knew."

"I haven't." She answered this readily.

"No need to tell me lies, just don't tell me the truth."

A flare of anger whipped through her. "I have never lied to you. I might have run away, but I've always been honest."

"You're right." He scrubbed his hand over his closely-shorn hair, and pain etched into his face. "I'm not . . . thinking clearly. I can't."

She moved closer. "The only man I yearned for was you. You're all I want. Kit. Please." She reached for him. "The dawn will come too soon."

She closed the distance between them, running her hands up his chest. His heart thundered beneath her palms. It matched the drumming of her own pulse.

For half a second he was still. Then, with a growl, he brought his arms around her, his hands cupping her behind, and hauled her close. He kissed her savagely. And when she met his wildness with her own, his approval was a tangible thing. Sound reverberated low in his chest. His cock thickened further, a column of steel against her belly.

Good god, had he actually grown bigger . . . there?

He moved his lips across her jaw, down along her neck. She shivered when his teeth scraped over her tender skin, his breath hot, and when he bit lightly on the curve of her shoulder, she moaned.

Impatient to feel more of him, she tugged at her chemise. He made faster work of her minimal clothing, whipping off her chemise and breaking the ribbon fastening of her pantalets so the fabric pooled at her feet. She kicked her pantalets away, and then she stood naked before him.

She reached for the buttons of his shirt, but he held her back gently. "Too soon. I need . . . *yes*." He brought her close again, one hand on her bare buttocks, the other cupping her breast.

He caressed her, his fingers circling her nipple, and it felt as though electricity fired through her, sparking in her breasts and lower, between her legs. Her nipples tightened into firm points. When he tugged on them, she gasped. Her pussy grew slick, aching. She ground against him. He was still fully clothed, while she was completely nude, and her arousal climbed higher from the contrast.

He moved his hand from her buttocks, stroking over her hip, over the curve of her belly. She couldn't hold back a long, low moan when his fingers dipped lower, and, when he discovered how wet she was, he growled.

She writhed against him as he continued to tease and pinch her nipples while his other hand stroked through the folds of her pussy. Each caress sent streaks of pleasure through her. His fingers were broad and calloused, his skin rough. Awareness dimmed. She knew only where he touched her, where he drew forth such fathomless pleasure.

He touched her with an expertise born from familiarity. He knew her body. Knew what she wanted, what she craved. He knew that pressing his thumb just *there* on her clit made her gasp, and he knew that sinking two fingers into her passage made her scream. And when he worked her, thumb on her clit, fingers thrusting in and out and pressing against that one exquisitely sensitive spot within, she felt his claim.

"Only I know you like this," he rumbled against her throat. "This is what I give you, Lulu. Me, and no one else."

"Kit, yes." Control burned away. She abandoned herself to pleasure, the pleasure he created.

The orgasm hit her with a tidal force. She threw her head back to scream her release, but his mouth on hers swallowed the sound. Surge after surge crashed over her, and he drove them on relentlessly, release after release, his hand locked intimately against and within her.

Finally, as her limbs shook and sweat coated her body, he took his hand away. One by one, he licked his fingers.

"As delicious as ever," he murmured.

Heavy lidded, she watched him, and it amazed her that, after so many climaxes, her desire burned just as bright.

"I need to know if you taste the same, too," she whispered.

His jaw looked made of stone as she slid down his body, then knelt before him, their gazes locked all the while. He moved just enough to grab the pillow from the berth and slide it under her knees.

"Always so considerate," she said with a wicked smile.

He seemed incapable of speech—a very good thing. He did growl, however, when she unfastened the buttons on his breeches. And when she reached in his drawers and pulled out his cock, the rough sounds he made were inhuman.

She took her gaze from his to stare at his cock. Her guess had been correct. His transformation had affected all parts of him. He was most assuredly bigger. Not that she'd had any cause for complaint before, but . . . well . . .

The wonders of science.

Hands clenched at his sides, he strained toward her. Yet she merely let her breath mist over him. She licked her lips, then rubbed them against the head of his cock. Moisture beaded at the tip, and when she licked her lips again, she tasted its saltiness.

"Lulu, damn it." His voice was a rumble.

It was time to end her play. She leaned closer and took him into her mouth.

Words that were half swears, half prayers tumbled from him.

The head was broad, and she ran her tongue around it before taking him deeper. She couldn't fit all of him in her mouth, so she gripped his shaft, pumping, as she sucked him. Oh, he tasted the same, male flesh and musk, and the feel and flavor of him stoked her excitement.

Tension vibrated through him. She felt him holding back, fighting to keep himself under control. Glancing up, she saw his eyes were tightly shut and the cords of his neck stood out as he struggled.

She pulled back. "Let go."

"I can't," he ground out.

"Kit. Look at me." When he pried his eyes open, blue fire in the darkness, she said, "I'm on my knees for you.

I'm giving you everything. And I want you to do the same for me."

He was still for a moment. Then, as though his bones had rusted, his hands slowly came up to cradle the back of her head.

"*Yes*," she whispered.

He guided her. She opened her lips, and his cock slid into her mouth. Yet she did not move. Simply waited.

His hips went back, then forward. She breathed in deeply, forcing herself to relax, as his cock filled her mouth completely, hard and thick. He moved again, thrusting into her mouth. She made a soft noise of arousal and encouragement. A noise that meant *More*.

With a growl, he gave her exactly that. His thrusts deepened. He held her immobile, hands and cock, and she closed her eyes as sensation pulsed in every part of her.

It was a kind of penance for the hurt she had caused, kneeling before him, allowing him to use her mouth so roughly for his own pleasure—but she did not feel subjugated by it. She knew her own power. It couldn't be touched. This moment was for him. And for her.

Opening herself to him like this, no sense of self, no will but the need to give and receive pleasure . . . her arousal knew no boundaries.

Of its own volition, her hand drifted between her legs. The other plucked at her nipple. She moaned around his cock. Almost at once, another climax tore through her.

His strokes grew quicker, his breathing ragged. Everything within him tensed. His own release loomed. His hands eased from around her head, and he moved as if to pull away, but she wouldn't allow it. Opening her eyes, she looked up and their gazes held. A question in his eyes. She answered it silently by keeping him in her mouth.

His body went rigid. A groan ripped from deep in his chest. His seed poured into her. Eyes closed in rapture, she swallowed—eliciting another groan from him.

He pulled out of her mouth and scooped her up in his arms. In two strides, he stood next to the bed and gently laid her down. She drifted for a moment, floating on echoing currents of sensation, and came back to awareness when she felt a wineglass pressed to her lips. Grateful, she sipped at the dark, rich wine. Eyes opened to slits, she watched as he drank wine as well, then set the glass aside. Drowsiness began to set in.

"Can't sleep yet," he cautioned with a wicked smile. "We've got more to do."

"But you . . ." She glanced down at his groin and was amazed to see that he was still just as hard and upright as he'd been before.

"Still want you." He pushed the braces off his shoulders and undid the buttons lining the front of his shirt. The shirt was dropped to the floor, and she saw again the astonishing musculature of his arms and torso, limned in starlight. The telumium implants gleamed on his shoulder.

He pulled off his boots, which thudded to the ground, and then stripped out of his breeches. He was naked.

She levered herself up on her elbows, no longer sleepy. The muscles of his thighs were thick and carved, his calves solid. And when he turned to shove all of their discarded clothing aside, she couldn't stop the gasp that sprang from her lips.

"You could charge admission to look at your arse." It was rock hard, with beautifully defined divots on each buttock.

He slanted her a grin. "Good to know I've a plan if my naval pension isn't enough."

Yet both of their smiles faded. They both seemed to realize at the same time that the prospect of a pension was unlikely. Neither of them believed they would survive the next twenty-four hours.

Lying back on the bed, she opened her arms to him. He went to her at once, sinuous and powerful, and stretched out beside her. The berth was narrow, but they pressed tight against one another, flesh to flesh. She always loved the contrast of their bodies, and now that the differences were even greater, she reveled in the sensation.

Braced on one elbow, he leaned over her. His fingers curved over the back of her neck, his thumb against the pulse drumming in her throat, and he kissed her deeply.

"I dreamed," he rumbled, "but never dared to hope. To have this with you again."

"Every night, I wished for you." She felt her heart in her gaze as she looked up at him. "It was my own fault I was alone, but that couldn't stop me from wanting. I would lie in my bed and ache to have you next to me, inside me. I'd touch myself and try to pretend it was you. Your hand on my skin. On my breasts. My sex. I'd come, crying your name."

His breathing became jagged, and he took her mouth again in a deep and searching kiss. She gripped his biceps, arching up to him.

"Did you think of me?" she whispered against his mouth. "Would you take your cock into your hand and stroke it, imagining it was my hand that gripped you? My pussy around you?"

As she spoke, she reached down and wrapped her hand around his cock, stroking him in time with her words. He groaned.

"Tried to deny myself," he said through his teeth. "So angry after you left. Tried to picture anyone else. That I was fucking some other woman."

She hadn't the means to be outraged over his confession. Her actions had been shameful.

"But I couldn't," he said. "It was you I imagined in my bed. No matter how hard I tried, I couldn't get you from my mind."

"Or your cock," she added, scraping her fingernails down his shaft.

He sucked in a breath. "Damned traitor—it wanted you even when my heart was bleeding."

"You can't know how sorry I am." Tears choked her throat. "For the suffering I caused us both."

"We'll not talk about that now." He stroked over her breasts, her belly, his touch both reverent and commanding. "These hours belong to the present, and I won't waste them on regret."

In response, she kissed him, sweeping her tongue into his mouth that she might drink him up. His tongue rubbed against hers, and they fell together into sensation, a long, liquid spiral.

Flames of need coursed through her. "I want more," she gasped. "I want you inside me. Where you've always belonged."

In a blur of movement, he shifted, kneeling between her legs. He gripped her hips, angling them up. The head of his cock nestled at her entrance. A heartbeat passed. He stared at her as though with sight alone he could devour her, and she gazed back as they shared a brief eternity. This was a ship of war, he himself was a weapon, but this . . . this was theirs.

He surged into her. A single, thick thrust. She bowed up with a cry, hands pressed to the bed. Ah, god, he filled her. Completely. Almost to the point of pain. But it was exquisite.

More sounds of ecstasy tore from her as he stroked in and out of her. Her pleasure climbed even higher, watching the flex and movement of his muscles, the metal on his shoulder supple and gleaming, as though some fantastic creature from ancient myth made love to her in the depths of night. And the noises he made verged on bestial, exciting her to madness.

She threw herself into the pleasure they made, pushing against the bed that she might take him further, deeper. Still, she wanted more.

As he did. He suddenly gathered her up, his arms supporting her beneath her buttocks, and stood. He was still buried deep within her as he strode to the bulkhead and braced her against it. With the bulkhead firm against her back, he sank even deeper into her. She cried out, and wrapped her legs around his waist.

"Wanted this," he growled. "So badly." He kept one arm supporting her from below, holding her up with his incomparable strength. With his other hand, he gripped her wrists, stretching her arms up over her head and pinning them to the bulkhead.

The posture sang with the truth: She was his. Unquestionably his. That had never changed.

"Kit," she moaned. "I love you."

His gaze flared with pleasure. He kissed her, hard, consuming her gasp as he thrust into her. Again and again, he sank into her welcoming depths, gaining speed and strength with each stroke. Here again, the benefits of his transformation, for he moved as no ordinary man could, piston-fast. Overwhelmed, lost to ecstasy, she could do nothing but feel, and what she felt was pleasure, devastating pleasure.

Release was incendiary. It utterly destroyed her. She bit down hard on his shoulder to muffle her scream. He snarled in approval. And as she came and came again, he continued to move, creating even greater pleasure.

Then the climax had him, and his whole body went rigid with release.

It could have been moments or years later when he let go of her wrists, and her arms slid bonelessly down. She barely had the strength to lift them so she could wrap them around his shoulders.

He carried her back to the bed, and there they lay down together. She draped over him. He cradled her close, murmuring wordless endearments against the crown of her head. It was almost like how it used to be after a night of intense lovemaking, when they would lie in each other's arms, drowsing and sated, content and secure.

She felt herself slipping into sleep. Never had she been more replete. But she couldn't feel content, nor secure. A perilous mission loomed just beyond the sunrise, and she could only wonder—had she found Christopher again, and the truth of her own heart, just in time to lose everything?

Chapter Nine

Sleep was for ordinary men. Since receiving his implants, Christopher had discovered that he needed less sleep. Three or four hours, rather than six or seven, were all he required to be at optimum capacity. At first, the change had been unsettling. By force of habit, he'd make himself get into his berth and stay there for the whole of the night. This became phenomenally dull, and he had soon begun to use those hours to write in his log or patrol the ship. Sometimes he even took the wheel from whoever had been assigned night watch.

After the chaos of his days, he'd started to enjoy the quiet and solitude of night, when the ship felt like his alone, and the canopy of stars seemed adorned for his private delight. It could be lonely, however, those long stretches of solitude, and those had been the hours when his thoughts had often turned to Louisa, reawakening a slumbering pain.

He was grateful now that he didn't need much sleep.

It meant he could bask in the pleasure of holding her one final night without a moment wasted.

She lay in his arms, softly asleep, her breath feathering across his chest. He wanted her again—but she needed her rest. And he wasn't entirely certain her body could withstand any more. That he hadn't hurt her seemed miraculous. Had she made the slightest sound of pain, he would have stopped immediately, agonizing though it might have been. Yet she'd reveled in him, in the almost brutal way he'd loved her. The bite mark on his shoulder ached pleasantly, evidence as to just how much she had enjoyed herself.

Brushing strands of hair from her face, he gazed down at her. At rest, the acuity of her usual expression fell away. She looked unguarded. Her sharp beauty softened. She seemed almost vulnerable.

She was both. Edged as well as vulnerable. He would never again make the mistake of believing she was simply one or the other.

She stirred, blinking up at him groggily. "Kit?"

"Shhh, love. Sleep." He pressed a kiss to her forehead.

Perhaps it was a measure of how he'd worn her out, for instead of insisting that she would stay awake, she promptly dozed off. Though when he drew the blanket up to cover her shoulder, she shrugged it away. Always had a mind of her own, even when sleeping.

He stared at the ceiling of his quarters, marking the subtle changes in light. Dawn would arrive soon, and with it, the most dangerous stage of the mission.

Fear for her clawed through him. She could protect

herself, could fight as ably as any trained sailor or soldier. But his was a primal fear. It couldn't be reasoned with or explained away. She was his. He wanted her safe.

She loved him.

God, hearing her say those words had been pure ether. His heart had soared, and even now, it felt as though it flew up amongst the constellations.

But he hadn't been able to say the words in return. She had demanded that he give her everything, as she gave him all of herself.

The words were there, filling his mouth with their shape and honeyed flavor. They couldn't move past his lips, however.

In the dark, he smiled, sardonic. This day would see him finding the enemy munitions plant and work to destroy it. A very good chance existed that he'd be killed in the process. Yet his two greatest fears had nothing to do with his death.

He feared for Louisa's safety.

And he feared the damage she could do to his heart.

He'd laid himself open to her three years ago, and the direct consequence had been unfathomable pain. Even with death looming close, and her sincere apologies, he couldn't fully trust her not to break his heart again. The lesson she'd taught him before had been too hard won.

Yet he had to wonder—how culpable had he been in her flight? She had been clear in her desire to avoid marriage, not merely to him, but to anyone. He'd asked for her hand anyway, convinced that he could change her mind. She had fled, but he'd driven her away, too.

He muttered a curse under his breath. Nothing was as simple as right or wrong, innocent or guilty. Only degrees of culpability.

Therein lay the beauty of a mission. It had a clarity of purpose. A direct goal. Find the munitions plant. Destroy it. He knew precisely what was required and how to go about executing the objective.

Love, however, was a rocky shore, full of uncertainty and hidden peril. No wonder so many men took to the sea or the skies. Easier when you knew the enemy would simply shoot at you, rather than sneak up with silken touches and then rip the beating heart from your chest, then tearfully apologize for the mortal wound.

He pushed all these thoughts from his mind. What he needed right now was clarity. He had only a few hours left with Louisa, and he fully intended to enjoy them for what they were. A beautiful woman slept in his arms, exhausted by their fiery lovemaking. She loved him. And he . . . cared deeply for her. That's as much as he could allow himself.

It would have to be enough.

STANDING AT THE forecastle of the ship, Christopher gazed at the chain of the dark, serrated mountains rising ahead. They looked like the black teeth of a huge beast, ready to clamp shut around the *Demeter* and make a quick meal of its crew. An unsettling thought for a ship's captain.

Louisa stood beside him, her spyglass trained on the mountains. Only hours earlier, they'd been naked in each other's arms. He still felt her there, the imprint of her body against his. Perhaps the last time he'd ever hold her.

He couldn't think of that now.

Her mouth formed a thin line beneath the lens. "No way to know which of those damned peaks is the one we want. Not from this distance. Can you see anything?"

"Just the tops of the mountains, which don't tell us anything. If we bring the ship closer, going from mountain to mountain, we'll be spotted long before we even find the right one." He gritted his teeth. "Hell. We can't use the train tracks leading out as a guide. There's got to be another way to figure out which of these houses our target."

He leaned against the rail and crossed his arms over his chest. "You're the explosives expert. If you had to pick one of these mountains as a place to assemble munitions, which would it be?"

"They all look the same." She snapped the spyglass shut. "And I've never built arms or explosives on a massive scale before. Components and chemicals, these I know. The construction of a weapons factory? That's outside of my bailiwick."

Frowning, he straightened. "Chemicals."

"The essential constituents of all explosives. Yesterday proved how specific the process needs to be. A single element out of place results in disaster." Her brow creased. "You're thinking something."

"The byproduct of the energy generated by my telumium implants is ether. It's the same with chemical reactions, too, isn't it? To create something, there are byproducts and excesses. Surplus and runoff."

Her eyes widened. "There are cloth mills that don't use tetrol or coal. They still rely on energy created by rivers to power their machinery. And the chemicals they use to dye the fabric wind up in the river. It runs all the way to the ocean, polluting the bay."

"But if you started in the bay," he said, his excitement growing, "or even farther up the river, you could follow those chemicals all the way to their source."

"Right to the factory itself. And a factory needn't use the river as its power to contaminate it, either. Chemicals are often either dumped or leech into nearby bodies of water." She gave an astonished laugh. "You've undervalued yourself, Kit."

Heat pulsed to life beneath his skin as he remembered her moaning that name—his name, shared only between them—as he'd buried himself in her. Color bloomed in her cheeks now, as well. Good. He didn't want her to forget a moment of what they'd shared.

But at this moment, what they needed to concentrate on was locating the munitions plant.

He pointed to the glint of water ribboning below. "Half a dozen rivers are fed by the mountains' snowmelt."

"Only one of them will take us to the factory. We're going to have to test each of them to find the one we want." Her mouth curved as she stared at the valley floor. "We've got a busy morning."

THE JOLLY BOAT skimmed over the treetops, its hull barely clearing the upper branches. As Christopher manned the tiller, he continually scanned the ground for signs of Hapsburg troops, or indeed anyone who might be alarmed to see an English boat flying above a Carpathian forest. Armed marines also kept lookout, one at the mounted swivel gun.

Louisa, too, had a rifle across her knees. She remained as vigilant as the rest of the boat's company. No one wanted to stumble into the hands of the enemy, not when they edged closer to gaining their objective. To have survived as much as they had, only to fall short at this juncture—it couldn't be allowed to happen.

Something gleamed ahead. Above the rushing wind came the laughter of running water. A river.

He dipped the jolly boat down below the treetops, slowing the vessel for its approach.

"Just ahead," he called over the wind. "Sharp eyes, everyone." Where there was a river, there could be troops provisioning or watering their horses. Or a local, terrified at the sight of a British Man O' War and red-coated marines.

The silver river twisted through the forest, and after a thorough scan of the area, Christopher landed the jolly boat on its wide, sandy bank. He held his hand up, a silent signal for everyone within the boat to wait before disembarking. If the enemy was near, he wanted to make certain that he, Louisa, and the marines could make a fast escape. He strained his sensitive hearing, searching for the tiniest sound—the snap of a twig, the creak of a leather strap—that might indicate soldiers were near.

A minute passed. Then another. He heard the lap

of water over rocks, the whirr of the jolly boat's small turbine, and faintly, the hum of the *Demeter*'s engines. Nothing else.

"It's secure," he said. "But no complacency, lads."

"Aye, sir," the marines answered.

Louisa had already unfastened her harness, and nimbly jumped over the side of the boat. Christopher handed the tiller to Farnley, then did the same. He trailed after her as she approached the river, his ether pistol in his hand and ready, his gaze continually sweeping the forest.

She crouched beside the moving water and studied it. A mosaic of pebbles lined the bed, and green river grass grew in patches. "Clear as glass. But that means nothing. Some of the deadliest poisons can't be seen, and there are chemicals that occur in such trace amounts that they are invisible without the aid of a microscope."

"Didn't bring my microscope," Christopher said, "though Dr. Singh might have one." Which would necessitate another trip back to the ship, slowing their progress.

"No need for such delicate equipment." To his surprise, she unfastened the first four buttons of her blouse, revealing the top of a plain cotton corset and the lacy edge of her chemise.

He shot a scowling glance toward the marines. The men promptly averted their gazes.

"This isn't the opportune moment for a bathe," he said lowly.

"Is it? I'd hardly noticed. The weather being so fine." She reached down the front of her bodice and tugged out a handkerchief. Fixing him with an exasperated look, she said, "A bit more faith in my judgment, if you please. This"—she dangled the handkerchief in front of him—"is treated with a chemical that changes color in the presence of different elements. If it's exposed to poison sulfur gas, it turns yellow. It'll change to green if it contacts the copper alloy the Hapsburgs use for their cannon shells. And if there's any trace of trinitrotoluene in the water, the fabric will turn red."

"And if there's no TNT?"

"Then the handkerchief simply gets wet."

He fought the urge to growl. "Mind doing up your blouse? It's been some time since my men have gone on leave." He himself was too distracted by the sight of her bare flesh.

"As though a few inches of my skin could drive them to a lustful frenzy." Still, she did as he asked. When she'd restored her clothing, she edged closer to the river. Holding the scrap of cambric by a corner, she dipped it into the water.

She held the handkerchief up. They both waited.

Its color remained the same. The river was free of TNT residue.

"Damn it." She wrung the kerchief out then stuffed it into her pocket. Standing, she muttered, "Never easy, is it?"

"There's no challenge in *easy*."

"I know how much you enjoy a challenge."

He followed her back to the waiting jolly boat. "That, I do."

THE PROCESS WAS repeated two more times: locate a river, test the water. In both instances, the tests revealed no signs of TNT, and thus no munitions plant.

It was their fourth expedition. As Christopher piloted the jolly boat closer to the next river, he forcibly tamped down on his impatience. He'd do nothing good by rushing this process. Every step was important. Yet he felt a small degree of satisfaction to see that Louisa's tolerance for the process also began to fray. If a spy with infinite reserves of patience was restive, then surely an airship captain more accustomed to battle might be forgiven for seething with frustration.

As he steered the jolly boat to the river, he noted that the trees grew too thick near the bank to land the vessel. The closest he could come was some fifty feet away, in a narrow clearing.

He brought the jolly boat down. "Farnley, Josephson, stay with the boat. Stone, Nizam, you're with me and Miss Shaw."

It was an indicator of Louisa's self-control that she managed to wait for him to issue his orders before leaping out of the boat. And though she cast eager glances toward the river, she lingered at the edge of the clearing rather than darting off on her own.

He took the lead, with Louisa following, and the two marines guarding the rear. The sheen of water appeared ahead, with narrow bands of sand forming banks. Before they broke from the trees, Christopher turned to Nizam and Stone.

"Stay back in the woods. Guard our backs."

"And your front, sir?" asked Nizam.

He laid his hand upon his ether pistol. "Taken care of."

The marines held back, arranging themselves to keep watch on the forest while Christopher and Louisa made for the river.

She waited for his nod before emerging from the trees. As she crouched, pulling out her treated handkerchief, he stood, his gaze alert and in motion.

A noise came from the other side of the river. Footsteps. He stiffened, his hand going for his pistol.

Louisa's shoulders tensed slightly as she caught the sound a second after him. "Wait," she whispered urgently. "Take off your coat. Bundle it up under your arm to hide your gun. Hurry."

Though he wanted to demand answers, he had to trust her in this. Quickly, he shucked his coat and covered his pistol with it. He didn't like obstructing his weapon, but his reflexes were fast enough. He could get to it in half a second if necessary.

"Make sure your men don't come out," she hissed.

He held up a hand, silently signaling the marines to stay back.

The footsteps drew closer. They moved in a shuffle, fallen pine needles soughing with each step.

"Hope you know what you're doing," he muttered. Glancing down at her, it took him a moment to recognize her. For with the subtlest shift in her expression, she transformed completely.

Gone was the sharp-eyed spy. In her place was a fresh-faced lass, almost ten years younger than Louisa's actual age. Her eyes were wide and guileless, her countenance smooth and untroubled. He had no idea how she accomplished this.

No time to wonder at this. An elderly man emerged from the forest on the other side of the river. Under his arm, he carried a basket. His other hand held a fishing pole. He wore a peasant's simple tunic, baggy pantaloons and an embroidered vest and boots. When he saw Louisa and Christopher, he started.

Louisa, too, made a show of surprise. She actually blushed. In a language Christopher couldn't understand, she said something to the old man. Even her voice had changed, sounding lighter, more girlish.

The elderly man's surprise faded, and he answered her in the same tongue. His gaze flicked to Christopher, growing cautious.

She spoke again. Laughter tinged her words, and a trill of feminine embarrassment. She made pretty gestures in the air, her hands like birds, thoughtless and lovely.

Whatever she said to the man, it made him chuckle. His response held notes of fond remembrance, as though he spoke of a pleasant time from long ago. This time, when he looked at Christopher, he winked.

Not knowing how to respond, Christopher returned the wink, and the man laughed again. He said something to Christopher.

"Just nod and say, *Merita riscul*," Louisa said, her voice pitched so softly that only Christopher could hear her.

He did as she directed, but when he repeated the words, the old man frowned.

"*El este din Ungaria,*" Louisa said at once.

The visitor nodded sagely. He gestured toward the river, seeming to indicate that he would take his fishing farther downstream.

"*Sper ca pestelle musca,*" Louisa said.

After a final wave, the elderly man picked his way along the riverbank, until he disappeared around a bend.

Christopher knew better than to start speaking English immediately. She understood, as well, continuing to chatter in that foreign tongue. As she did, she dipped the handkerchief into the water.

A moment later, the square of cambric turned red.

This was the river they sought, the one that would lead them to the munitions plant.

Still, Louisa did not leap up. She wrung out the handkerchief and dabbed it on her face—though his acute sight revealed that she did not, in truth, actually touch the fabric to her skin. Then, as if she had all the time in the world and didn't care at all about the location of the munitions plant, she stood and took hold of his arm. She nuzzled close.

"I told him my parents didn't approve of you, a Hungarian who cannot speak Romanian very well, thus your accent." Her whisper curled warmly in his ear. "We'd come here for a tryst and were, ah, tidying up before you escorted me partway home."

"Let's ensure our disguise." He turned his head and kissed her, as a man might kiss his lover, uncertain of their next meeting. Which was a fiction all too easy for him to believe.

He knew the marines watched from the trees, and couldn't bring himself to care. For a hand's-breadth of time, he and Louisa had each other. With the location of the plant almost revealed, the greatest danger lay ahead.

She kissed him deeply, her lips telling him that she also knew of the imminent peril, and clung to these moments with a shared hunger.

He and Louisa broke apart. She continued to hold his arm as they moved back into the woods. Neither he nor she blinked when the red-faced marines joined them for the rest of the walk to the jolly boat. Hell, he might be dead by the end of the day, and his command of his ship was never in doubt. So he met the marines' embarrassed gazes without a trace of shame. Doubtful that anyone wondered at his relationship with Louisa. He knew how he looked at her.

And the way she looked at him . . . He couldn't stop the clench of heat at the possessiveness in her gaze.

"Nicely played," he said. "The performance back there. You became someone else."

"Missed my calling as a stage actress. But the rage is for automatons now, anyway, so I ought to stay with spying. It's more secure work than the theater."

"And the conditions less dangerous."

They reached the jolly boat, where Farnley and Josephson waited. "We've found our target," Christopher said. He moved to help Louisa back into the small vessel, but she had already climbed in, agile as a riddle. She might look at him with desire, perhaps even love, yet she remained her own woman, self-sufficient and capable.

At Christopher's pronouncement, the marines brightened, eager to reach their objective.

"Back to the *Demeter*, sir?" Farnley asked.

"Aye. And then we strike at the Huns' heart." He vaulted into the boat and took up his position at the tiller.

Once everyone had buckled themselves in, he brought the boat up. They rose above the trees, branches brushing against the hull and scattering needles upon the floor. He was careful to keep the boat out of sight of the old man, lest the fellow happen to look up and see an English jolly boat flying through the air.

They joined the *Demeter*, coming up through the cargo doors in her keel. Pullman and Herbert waited there, and the moment Christopher killed the jolly boat's engine, he was out of the vessel and issuing orders.

"Chart us a course up the river, Mr. Herbert. Mr. Pullman, spread word to the crew." He strode into the passageway, followed by Herbert, Pullman, and Louisa. "We're on the trail. All unnecessary activity is to be kept to a minimum. We've got the enemy in our sights, lads, and can't leave anything to chance."

"Aye, sir." Pullman and Herbert saluted and broke away to carry out their orders.

Without speaking, Christopher and Louisa progressed to his quarters. It had been cleaned since last he'd been inside, the berth made. The mattress and pillows no longer bore the indentations from two sleepers. It was almost as it had been before she had come onto his ship. But the air itself had altered, charged with her presence, and faintly scented with jasmine.

He stepped inside briskly, going straight to the plan for the munitions plant spread upon the table. She stood on the other side of the table, also studying the drawing.

"Here, here, and here." She pointed to different locations. "These are the places we'll need to position the bombs. The explosions will breach the security walls, setting off anything combustible within. Should bring the whole place down."

"We'll break into three teams, get the bombs situated faster."

She shook her head. "Security is going to be tight. Two people might barely be able to slip in undetected. Any more and the risk increases. It'll be me, and whomever from your crew you can spare."

He stared at her. "Whomever I can spare? The hell kind of talk is that? *I'm* going with you."

"But . . ." She looked patently confused. "You're the ship's captain. They'll need you here."

"The most important part of this mission is getting the bombs planted. The factory has to be destroyed." He folded his arms across his chest. "There are only two people I'm certain can accomplish that. You. And me."

"What about the ship?"

"Pullman can look after the *Demeter* while I'm gone. If the ship manages to survive, but I don't, she's got enough ether stored to make it back to neutral territory."

She stalked around the table. "They don't just need you as a fuel source. They need you as a captain."

"My greatest responsibility is ensuring that this operation is a success." When she started to object further, he said, more quietly, "And I don't entrust your safety to anyone but me."

Her protests abruptly silenced. For a moment, she only gazed at him, then she lifted up on her toes and kissed him. Tenderly.

Her smile was self-deprecating as she pulled back slightly. "I wouldn't trust me, either."

"I do," he said at once.

"With the mission. But not your heart." She pressed her hands to the center of his chest. "I tell you this: If we do make it out of this place alive, I'm going to earn your trust again."

He covered her hands with his own, feeling their slim strength. The river water had chilled her fingers, but the heat from his body chased away lingering cold.

She said, "I love you."

Only a few minutes ago, she'd hidden herself behind the identity of a simple country girl. Now, there was no disguise. No subterfuge. She was completely open. Entirely herself. Only for him.

Her gaze held his. Searching. "I know you can't say it back to me. Not yet."

He couldn't deny this. Words formed and dissolved before they reached his mouth. He wanted to speak, aware of their time together ticking away and the threat that loomed. But he couldn't feed her half-truths. He couldn't promise her that he'd say the words she wanted some time in the future. There might not be a future. So he kept silent.

Chapter Ten

DEATH LOOMED ON the horizon. It revealed itself in the huge form of a mountain, dark and jagged, stretching up toward a pristine blue sky. It was part of a chain of mountains forming a serrated undulation, yet it stood out from its stone-shouldered companions due to its size. An air of cruelty seemed to cling to its rough surface, threats crouching amidst the shadows dotting its face.

A fanciful notion. Studying the mountain through her spyglass, Louisa understood objectively that it couldn't exude malice. A mountain had no feelings, no objectives or loyalties. Yet knowing that weapons against Britain were being manufactured within the stone walls, she couldn't stop the cold unease that slid across her heart.

She turned at the sound of Christopher's boots upon the deck behind her. He strode up, grim-faced, and stood next to her at the forecastle rail.

"There." He pointed to a spot about three miles farther down the chain of mountains. Two peaks formed a small shelter that would be hidden from the mountain housing the munitions plant. "That's where the *Demeter* will deposit us. You and I will make the rest of the way on foot."

It was a sound plan. Only a madman would attempt to breach a heavily-guarded enemy position from the ground, and with no more firepower than an ether pistol. Which meant that that was precisely the means by which she and Christopher would gain entrance.

"Good thing I've got sturdy boots." None of those delicate kidskin confections most ladies favored would stand up to a three-mile hike, with row upon row of miniscule buttons and soles as thick as calling cards. "And will the *Demeter* rendezvous with us at the same spot?"

"By that point, subterfuge won't be an option. We'll have to signal the jolly boat when we get out. Then it will wait for us in the forest as close to the factory gates as it can get."

Neither she nor Christopher voiced what she knew they were both thinking. It was highly unlikely that either of them would be alive to signal the jolly boat. A plan was needed, however, should that slim chance come to pass. Only amateurs operated without a plan.

They gazed at one another a moment. All around was the sky, the activity of the ship, yet on the forecastle, and in her heart, she and Christopher were alone.

Her hand found his. "I shouldn't be so selfish, glad you'll be down there with me, instead of with your ship."

His blue eyes were more dazzling than the sky. "There's nowhere I'd rather be." He pressed his palm to hers, warm and large, the most capable hands she'd ever known.

He was all she could hope for.

"Come," she said. "We haven't much time. Let's get ourselves rigged up." Their hands broke apart as they stepped down from the forecastle. She led him to the magazine and gestured to the object sitting upon the worktable. "We needed a way to transport the bombs that left both of our arms free, in case we encounter resistance. So I made that. It's not elegant, but it should get the job done."

He stepped forward and examined her handiwork. She had taken a section of the slotted wooden racks lining the magazine, sized to hold cannon shells, and attached two leather straps to it. The bombs were already fitted into the rack, waiting their destructive purpose.

Christopher slipped his arms through the straps. He tested the give of the straps, ensuring that he had freedom of movement.

"A rack becomes a pack." He nodded, satisfied. "Has a good symmetry."

"Poetic, too."

Other weapons were arranged for their use, and she and Christopher were silent as they armed themselves. Louisa slid an ether pistol into the holster around her waist. Christopher did the same. They each buckled on cartridge belts, and she carried a pack with additional ammunition. They checked to ensure that the small ether tanks on their weapons were full. The guns could still function without the ether, but having the gas's additional force gave the weapons far more firepower.

In the middle of her preparations, she glanced up to watch Christopher arm himself. His movements were quick, practiced, efficient. There was no fear or uncertainty in his face. He was a seasoned veteran, a warrior in every way.

There was a rightness in this. In preparing herself for her most dangerous mission, knowing that Christopher would be with her every step of the way.

He caught her glance, and his own flared with understanding. And heat. It never went away, the desire between them, no matter what perils loomed close.

His gaze moved over her, stirring warmth wherever it alit. He strode to her and tipped her mouth up to his for a deep, thirsty kiss. "I like you like this," he murmured. "Windblown, beautiful. Armed to the teeth."

"An unusual aesthetic you have, Captain."

"It gives me no cause for complaint."

The lightness of their talk was a thin muslin sheet drawn over the hulking form of upcoming danger. It barely disguised its shape, its size, but for a brief moment, she and Christopher could pretend it wasn't in the chamber with them.

There were better uses of their time than talking, so she pulled him down again for another kiss. She tasted their mutual need, felt their shared striving to hold on to something transient. No matter how they pressed close, his long hard body tight against her, the broad span of his hands at her waist, their mouths hungry and demanding, time slipped away.

A small cough sounded at the door to the magazine.

They broke apart, both turning to find a red-faced Pullman standing in the passageway just outside.

"We're in position, sir."

Christopher's hand remained on her waist as he spoke. "Thank you, Mr. Pullman."

The first mate gave a salute, and drifted away, leaving them alone.

Louisa raised a brow. "Surprised you didn't know he was there, with that sharp hearing of yours."

His grin came fast as sunlight. "Who says I didn't hear him?"

Before she could formulate a response, he bent down and gave her one final kiss, shattering in its tenderness.

Then it was over. Blue, blue eyes stared into hers. "Ready?"

She drew in a breath, steadying herself. In the whole of her service to the Navy, she never backed down from a mission, no matter its risks. This would be no different.

"Let's win this war."

Together, they left the magazine. They walked through the passageway, moving through the ship, heading down to the cargo bay.

Tension blanketed the ship as they progressed through it, the crew largely silent, every man aware that these next few hours meant not only success or failure, but life or death. Yet the crew went about their duties with straight shoulders, determination radiating from them.

Moving down from deck to deck, everyone saluted as she and Christopher passed by. Gravely, she nodded at each man. She couldn't help but think of their salutes as funereal rites. The ship might survive the mission. She and Christopher would not.

"You've earned their loyalty," she said quietly as more crew appeared in the passageway, saluting.

"I've given them what they deserve. Respect your crew, and you're repaid in kind." He tilted his head at the crewmen, who drew up straighter, gratified at his notice.

That was Christopher: a man who was fiercely loyal, but only to those who earned his loyalty. She'd spoken truly earlier—she could not fault him for being guarded with her. She could only hope that she'd go to her death having earned back at least a fragment of his trust.

Reaching the cargo bay, she found Pullman, Dr. Singh, and several other officers waiting. Surprisingly, Duffy the cook was also there. He handed her a small linen-wrapped bundle.

"Some *sables de citron*, should you find yourself hungry."

"No other saboteur is so well provisioned." She took the bundle and carefully packed it into her haversack. "My thanks, Mr. Duffy."

The cook ducked his head and gave her a shy smile.

Christopher was in quick, quiet consultation with Pullman and the officers, discussing in low voices his plans and what he expected of them should he be killed during the ground operation. Everyone wore matching tense expressions, especially the first mate. It was clear he'd rather Christopher commanded the ship, but he seemed ready to take up his duty.

"Send Farnley and Josephson in the jolly boat for us

in two hours," Christopher said. "If we're not there, the marines are to wait no more than fifteen minutes before returning to the ship. Under no circumstances are they to wait longer than a quarter of an hour. Understood?"

"Aye, sir."

Tydings, the bosun, pulled the lever on the cargo doors. Gears ground together as the doors swung open, and the cargo bay filled with an upsweep of cold wind. Below was the rocky face of the mountainous drop-off point, some hundred feet down. Tydings knotted one end of a very long coiled rope to an upright support beam. The bosun tugged hard on the rope, testing the strength of the knot. He nodded to Christopher.

At the captain's signal, Tydings dropped the rope out the cargo doors. It unspooled, whipping down, down. Until it dangled above the earth. There still looked to be thirty feet between the end of the rope and the ground. The rope itself whipped in the wind, looking as stable as a snake.

Pullman spoke into the shipboard auditory device. "Can you get us any lower?"

"No, sir," came the tinny voice on the other end of the line. "Not without possibly damaging the hull."

"I don't need her lower," Christopher said. "The jump won't prove a difficulty."

"For *you*," Louisa answered. There seemed no place where she might make a safe rolled landing if she had to fall the rest of the distance.

"Leave the jump to me," he said.

She wouldn't question him in front of his men, so she only nodded. He strode to the edge of the open cargo doors to stand beside the dangling rope. The ground looked very far away. He appeared not the slightest bit concerned.

He bent to grab hold of the rope, but stopped and straightened. Facing his officers, he said, "It's been an honor serving with you men."

Every crewman in the cargo bay saluted. He returned the salute. With his long blue coat, polished boots and look of pride for his men, Christopher could have served as a recruiting placard for the Navy. God knew Louisa would follow him anywhere.

He dropped his salute and gathered up several lengths of the rope, gripping it with his hands. He glanced at Louisa.

"Your ferry awaits," he said.

She stood next to him, trying not to gaze down at the distant ground below, nor the sharp rocks jutting up. There were no soft landings.

She looped her arms around his neck, then gripped her wrists in a secure hold. It looked like an intimate embrace, save for the fact that they stood beside open cargo doors and were both strapped down with weapons and explosives. If he lost his grip and plunged to the ground, the impact would set off the bombs. Not only would she and Christopher be killed instantly, but the *Demeter* would be caught in the explosion and torn apart. Thus the mission would end before it had truly begun.

Fear must be pushed away. She refused to have anything to do with it. When an agent began to doubt herself, she opened the door to disaster.

"I'm ready," she said.

He looked at her for a moment, as though committing

her face to memory. Then he lowered them both to the floor of the cargo hold. Their legs dangled down. Cold wind rushed up her skirts and swirled around her legs like a frigid, searching hand. At least she wore woolen stockings to keep the cold at bay. But catching pneumonia was the least of her concerns.

"Look at me," he commanded.

Her gaze snapped back to his face. The face she knew as well as her own—perhaps even better, for she'd spent many more hours contemplating his face rather than hers.

When he seemed satisfied that he had her full attention, he pushed off the floor of the cargo hold. And then they spun in midair. High above the rock-strewn, sloping ground.

Hand beneath hand, he climbed down the rope. He moved smoothly, showing no strain from her weight. The wind pulled at them, icy as it scraped down from the snow-covered peaks, and the farther away they went from the hull of the ship, the more the rope snapped and danced. Even Christopher's considerable weight couldn't keep it fully anchored. She felt like a fish at the end of a line. Dizzy, she closed her eyes and laid her head against his shoulder.

But curiosity wouldn't allow her to keep her eyes shut. She opened them again to watch him as he climbed lower and lower, the ground nearing in steady degrees. Craning her neck, she looked up to see the keel of the *Demeter* above, and the open cargo doors. Faces gathered around the doors, watching as she and Christopher went down, down.

She looked back down. For a few moments, she forgot

to be frightened, feeling the strength of Christopher's body and the pleasure of flight. A strange, giddy bubble rose in her chest. Her cheeks hurt. She thought she might be smiling.

Her smile faded, however, when they reached the end of the rope, and still thirty feet stood between them and the ground.

"Now what?" she called above the wind.

"A leap of faith." With one hand still holding the rope, he scooped his other arm beneath her, cradling her to him.

The only thing keeping them aloft was his hand gripping the rope.

And then he let go.

The ground rushed up to meet them, a blur of gray. She decided it wouldn't be cowardly to close her eyes once more.

Impact suddenly rattled through her. It jolted her bones. But the impact was far less than if she'd attempted the jump herself.

She cracked her eyes open to see that Christopher had landed in a crouch. He rose to standing, still holding her, betraying no signs that he was in pain or had injured himself. The wonder of his transformation continued to unfold.

Carefully, he set her on her feet.

"Hurt?"

"A bit wobbly from the excitement, but everything's in working order." Solidity returned to her legs in gradual degrees.

He waved at the ship, still hovering overhead. Though

she couldn't discern the tiny figures of the men looking out of the cargo hold, one of them must have spotted Christopher's signal, for the rope was drawn up. The *Demeter* rose higher, then flew off to find a hiding spot. The hum of its engines faded as the airship disappeared between the mountains.

Louisa and Christopher were alone.

A brief moment was taken to gather their bearings. They stood near the base of one mountain, just above the scree slope. Thick-trunked trees massed around the foot of the mountain. The only sounds came from the wind in the treetops and scattered birdsong.

"An ideal place for a picnic," she said.

"We'll have to come back with some wine and bread. Spread a blanket out beneath that tree."

They both knew no such thing would ever happen, but it made for a pleasant diversion as they collected themselves. Or rather, as Louisa composed herself, for he looked as unruffled as if he'd stepped off the front step of the Officers' Club rather than climbed down seventy feet of rope with a woman hanging from his neck, then jumped another thirty feet.

She pulled out her pocket watch. Their two hours had already begun.

In silent agreement, they edged their way down the scree as quickly as the treacherous gravel slope would allow. Then they were in the forest, the trees silent and immobile sentries as she and Christopher jogged through the woods. His long coat flew out behind him as he ran, like the wings of a great, dark bird.

Though she kept herself well-conditioned for situations exactly like this one, Christopher clearly had to slow his stride so she might keep up with him. It was only moderately annoying. She'd taken several trophies in running when at school.

"How fast can you run?"

"Haven't measured it."

"Hazard a guess."

"Forty, forty-five miles an hour."

She shook her head. "Your boots would fall apart before you did."

In all ways he was extraordinary. But he had been this way well before his transformation into a Man O' War.

They fell silent and continued their run toward the munitions plant. All unnecessary communication had to be curtailed the closer they got to the enemy's position, and she needed to conserve her breath for when she truly needed it. For over half an hour, they ran, dodging between trees, jumping over fallen trunks, careful to keep their footfalls as quiet as possible. Easy for Christopher, not as easy for her.

Yet she did not slow or falter. Only sped along as quickly as she could. The longer it took to reach the munitions plant, the less time she'd have to plant the bombs and attempt to flee before they detonated.

Christopher stopped abruptly, just at the edge of the forest. She skidded to a halt beside him.

Eyes wide, she beheld their objective. One hundred feet ahead. The munitions plant.

As the plans had suggested, the back wall was indeed

carved from the side of a mountain. The front of the plant jutted out, built from stone that must have come from the mountain itself. Its imposing façade was five stories high, with small square windows spaced at uneven intervals. There was nothing beautiful about the structure, no attempts at ornament. It was aggressive in its austerity. It served only one purpose: to build weapons to be used against the enemy.

The enemy was her. And Christopher. And the whole of Britain.

There were only two entrances. The one closest to Louisa and Christopher's position had to be where the workers entered and left. It was the size of a normal doorway, with a heavy steel door. A path had been worn into the ground from the tread of many feet. Sentries armed with ether rifles guarded the door. Clearly, a direct approach to this door was out of the question.

The second entrance was situated at the other end of the plant. Two massive sliding doors, with two sets of train tracks, marked where shipments came and went from the factory. This entrance was just as guarded as the one for the workers. One couldn't simply slip past the sentries, not without attracting notice.

Because the train was one of the plant's more vulnerable areas, much of the forest had been cleared away around the tracks' approach to the factory. If anyone attempted to hop onto the train, they'd be spotted by the guards and shot.

It would take a hell of a lot of calculation and a considerable amount of luck to get inside.

Fortunately, she and Christopher had a goodly share of cunning. He silently gestured to her, and they both faded back into the forest. They had one hope of breaching the munitions plant.

"Train's coming soon," he whispered to her. They would need to move quickly.

It seemed counterintuitive to get into the factory by walking away from it, but this was the only means of getting inside. They followed the sound of water—the very river they had used to track the location of the factory. Emerging from the trees, they found themselves standing at the top of a gorge. A trestle bridge traversed the gorge, with train tracks running the length of the bridge.

The gorge was deep, and the trestle bridge high. Its steel-beamed structure soared up fifty feet in a complex geometry. Where the tracks met up with the land had also been denuded of trees, leaving no cover for anyone who might try to climb aboard the train. Which meant there was a single location where a potential stowaway might climb on: from the trestle bridge itself.

Already the sounds of the approaching train filled the gorge. Fortunately the train would be running at a slow speed as it approached the munitions plant. Had it traveled at its normal velocity, anyone attempting to board via the underside of the train would be crushed. Even so, it would be a difficult, dangerous process.

First, she and Christopher must reach the train.

After a silent exchange, they scrambled down into the gorge. Christopher's implants gave him the nimbleness of a mountain cat, easily leaping from outcropping to outcropping. She hadn't the same technological advantage, and made her way down at a slower pace. Only a few times did she slip, scraping her hands against the rocks, and only a few times muttering to herself about lucky bastards enhanced by telumium.

At last she reached the bottom of the gorge, where Christopher waited for her. He frowned over the abrasions on her hands, yet there wasn't time to do any field dressing. The wounds were minor, so she shrugged them off, and both she and Christopher hurried toward the base of the trestle bridge. They waded through the icy river, which rushed up to their knees and made her skirts tangle.

Some women in England had adopted wearing trousers—mostly factory women who were more concerned about earning their wages than societal opinion. There was good sense in abandoning skirts for trousers. If she made it out of this mission alive, she'd definitely look into getting a few pairs for herself.

They reached the bottom of the trestle and stared up at their next obstacle, rising up into the afternoon sky. She swallowed hard, battling back another surge of trepidation.

"Ferry service down and ferry service up," he said as she looped her arms around his neck.

"I had no idea Man O' Wars offered such a wide variety of amenities." She angled herself so that she hung from his side, leaving his front free and staying off the pack with the bombs on his back. It wasn't the most comfortable situation, but she hadn't been recruited to Naval Intelligence with promises of comfort.

At her nod of readiness, he grasped the bars of the trestle and began to climb the inside of the bridge supports. She felt the flex and give of his muscles, the incredible strength of his body. Pressed this close, she also saw the fire of determination in his gaze as he ascended, his focus trained entirely on this task.

"If we weren't so damned expensive to create," he said, "we could replace all the locomotives and tetrol-powered engines." He didn't sound out of breath at all, despite the fact that he climbed up a huge trestle with a full grown woman and a complement of weaponry clinging to him.

She helped where she could, using her heels to push against the metal bars to propel them upward. The ground shrank away as they climbed higher, the river diminishing. If Christopher let go, or something knocked him off the trestle, the shallow water would provide no cushioning for their fall. They'd dash their brains out on the rocky river bottom, and the water would turn red then pink with their blood. If the bombs didn't blow them to ashes.

"Not just a matter of expense." She talked to distract herself. "Only a few men have the *aurora vires* ratings high enough to become Man O' Wars."

"No need to limit it to just half the populace."

Her brows rose. "Women, too?"

"Everyone's got an *aurora vires*. There could be women who rank Gimmel or higher. Maybe even you." He grabbed the next higher bar, pulling them upward.

"Female Man O' Wars. Interesting thought." She

pushed against the bars for more propulsion. "And if we turned rogue, like some Man O' Wars do, we could become a tribe of Amazons."

"Don't." He paused for a brief moment, his gaze holding hers. "Even if they offer you the choice, don't become like me."

The gravity in his eyes surprised her. "You've so many advantages." Strength, for one.

"The cost is damned high." He resumed climbing.

She wondered what that cost might be, but now wasn't the time to press him for answers.

A train whistle sounded, and the trestle rumbled with the locomotive's approach.

Christopher climbed faster, until they were just below the tracks. The ground was very far below, so she kept her attention on the bridge. It was supported by vertical posts, with angled sway braces shoring up the posts and providing additional stability. If she and Christopher attempted to climb the outside of the trestle and then clamber onto the oncoming train, they'd be spotted by the patrol gliders or the sentries.

"The best way on is from below," he said.

"Below?" That would entail him swinging from the post and grabbing hold of the beam running down the middle of the track. Even without the additional burden of Louisa and the bombs, it was a feat no normal man could accomplish.

But Christopher wasn't a normal man.

He heard the doubt in her voice and grinned. "Climbing the rigging was always one of my favorite things to do on a ship. Used to swing from them like a damned monkey. This won't be much different."

She had to trust his confidence. After drawing a breath, she nodded.

The trestle shook even harder as the train reached it. It moved slowly, yet the whole bridge shuddered with its movement. Many tons of machinery hissed and growled overhead, metal wheels turning, and through the gaps in the support slats, she saw the underside of the cargo carriages, and its network of struts and rails.

He drew in a breath, readying himself. She felt his body coil, like a predator about to strike, and then—

They flew through the air. A moment's weightlessness.

His hands closed around the central support bar. Jolted, she fought to keep her own grip. Her arms ached. Yet she hung on.

And so did he. She watched with amazement as he pulled them both up using the strength only of his arms. A sudden flash of remembrance from the night before, when he'd held her effortlessly against the bulkhead of his cabin and thrust into her.

She shook her head to clear it. Good god, what a thoroughly inappropriate thought to have at this moment. Yet a deep, feminine part of her thrilled to witness again his colossal strength. As if he read her mind, he gave her a wicked smile.

His smile faded, however, when they contemplated their next task. They hung from the central support beam, and while there was enough room between the cross ties to slip through, they'd have to move very quickly to grab the undercarriage. A false move could cause them to slip and fall across the tracks.

"On my count," he said through gritted teeth. "One, two, three—now!"

She moved upward between the ties. Then wrapped her hands around one of the metal struts running beneath the carriage. She swung her legs up at almost the same time and hooked her heels into another strut. Her arms, already tired from holding on to Christopher, shook. She wasn't going to be able to hang on long enough.

Suddenly, he was beside her. He used the side of his chest and one arm to keep her up, and his boots found purchase on the same strut where she'd positioned her feet.

"It's all right," he spoke above the clatter of the train. "I've got you."

Turning her head, she caught a glimpse of the track scrolling beneath them—his pack containing incredibly potent explosives was mere inches from the ground. Within a moment, they'd crossed the bridge and were on solid ground. She recognized the rocky terrain that surrounded the munitions plant's exterior. Though the train was moving very slowly, its din was terrific, filling her head with the clatter of wheels and the hiss of its breaks.

Good lord, they had done it! More to the point, Christopher had done it. Without his Man O' War abilities, they never could have succeeded in this outrageous scheme.

They were on the train, but could they get inside the

munitions plant? She saw sentries' boots moving close to the train. The guards examined every carriage as they rolled past, sliding open the doors on the freight cars and checking inside to make certain no one was infiltrating the plant.

A sentry approached the car to which she and Christopher clung. The guard pulled open the door and peered into it. She held her breath, waiting. Any moment now, and the sentry would look under the car and find them there. She'd no doubt that they would be shot first, long before an interrogation.

The guard moved on. They hadn't been seen.

Her breath released in a rush, and she saw Christopher's brief smile.

The train rolled on. It passed through the open doors. Sunlight vanished, replaced by the yellow glare of sodium lights. They rolled deeper into the factory, freight platforms on either side of the tracks.

Finally, the train stopped. Christopher didn't let go, not for several minutes. Workers shouted to one another, but only to call out instructions or complain about the frequency with which they had to fill up the ever-demanding trains. No one came to drag her and Christopher out from under the train. No ether rifles poked their muzzles below to unleash a torrent of bullets.

They had done it. They were inside the munitions plant.

She whispered to Christopher, "Now comes the challenging part."

Chapter Eleven

CHRISTOPHER THOUGHT IT a miracle that they'd made it this far. But he wasn't about to let Louisa know that.

Carefully, he released his grip on the undercarriage struts. It might take more than a jolt from some train tracks to detonate the bombs he carried, but he didn't want to test that theory. So he gently lowered himself and Louisa to the ground, protecting both her and the explosives.

The space between the underside of the car and the tracks wasn't quite big enough to allow him to crouch. Both he and Louisa remained on their hands and knees, waiting to be certain no sentries or other factory workers appeared. It would be damned ludicrous if he and Louisa made it this far, only to be caught by a laborer ambling around in search of his tea.

When it appeared safe, he gave her a nod. But not before pressing a quick kiss to her lips. She'd impressed the hell out of him with her courage. Even if he'd done the heavy lifting, not many women and hardly any men would have been able to endure the rigors of jumping from an airship, a three-mile run through the forest, scrambling down a gorge, hanging on for a rigorous climb up a trestle bridge, and then clinging to a moving train. All while evading the enemy.

She seemed to understand the significance of his kiss, for her eyes gleamed with pleasure.

Then it was time to move. They crept out from beneath the train and crouched next to the loading platform. Empty wooden pallets awaited munitions to be loaded onto the train. A typewriter sat upon a battered wooden desk, with a quartz lamp providing minimal light.

"Looks deserted," he whispered.

"For now."

"Let's not wait for the evening rush." He pulled himself up onto the platform, and she followed. They both hunkered low, alert to any sign of someone approaching.

He nodded toward an open doorway leading off of the cargo loading area. "That was on your plans."

"It'll take us where we need to go."

Straightening, they both hurried toward the door and then found themselves in a long, door-lined corridor. Overhead, sodium lights buzzed, giving everything a jaundiced, sickly look.

"This way." Louisa hurried ahead.

He followed, continually glancing over his shoulder to be certain no one saw them or pursued. Though the munitions plant was filled mostly with workers, any of them might sound an alarm to summon armed guards, or else try to play hero and attempt to subdue him and Louisa.

She reached the end of the corridor and flattened herself against the wall, peering around the corner to see if anyone was there. He stood close to the wall, as well, careful not to rattle the bombs strapped to his back.

At the sound of approaching footsteps, they both pressed back, keeping hidden.

A group of six plant workers walked down a perpendicular hallway. They wore heavy waxed canvas aprons. Though Christopher didn't know the language they spoke, the tired chatter of factory employees complaining of long hours or supervisors never varied. Too immersed in their own dissatisfaction, none of the workers cast a glance toward him or Louisa. Someone made what must have been a joke, for the others chuckled ruefully, and they walked on.

She waited several moments before moving on.

Impatience seethed within him, both as a Man O' War and as a man more comfortable with action than subterfuge. "Not used to this kind of skullduggery," he muttered.

She cast him a rueful smile and whispered, "A straight up fight in the sky is what you do best. But sneaking around down here is what *I* do best." She patted him on the hand. "Buck up, Captain. We may yet get a nice brawl."

"A cheering thought."

Seeing that they were in the clear, she slid into the next corridor. He was right behind her. Though he'd looked at the plans for the munitions plant many times, she clearly had memorized them, for she moved quickly and with precision. The factory was a maze of hallways, sodium lights, and doors.

Clear glass tubes ran along the ceiling. They spread out in a network, running into different rooms, and they emitted a faint hissing sound. Periodically, brass cylinders shot through them, heading in sundry directions.

"Pneumatic tubes," Louisa whispered. "Sending messages throughout the factory. Much faster than sending a courier."

"And they keep the hallways clear." Which was good for him and Louisa. Fewer messengers meant fewer people in the corridors, and less chances of being spotted.

Flaking metallic numerals had been painted upon the doorways. Louisa seemed to be searching for one in particular, for she rejected several doors before finally opening one.

They stepped inside and shut the door behind them. The room was dark and echoing. She fumbled in her pack for a moment. A small circle of green light bloomed as she held up a quartz lantern. They both cursed softly as they beheld the contents of the chamber.

It was a vast storage room. Racks soared up, stretching beyond the quartz lantern's minimal illumination. On the racks were countless wooden crates. He strode to one and pried up its lid. Inside, packed in straw, munitions lay like sleeping animals.

He pushed the lid back into place. They walked further into the storage chamber, passing more racks. Suddenly, several of the racks began to shake.

His ether pistol was out in an instant, as was Louisa's. It might have been some kind of alarm system; they needed to be prepared if anyone came running.

Cautiously, he neared one of the shuddering racks. Its shaking increased the closer he came. Instead of crates on the rack, there were sheets of metal stored upright. Pegs held them in place. The metal trembled at his approach.

He pressed his hand flat against one of the sheets. "Telumium." He felt it resonating through his shoulder and his body.

"It's responding to you." She stepped closer and frowned. "I heard no intelligence that they were making Man O' Wars here. What purpose could all this telumium serve?"

He resisted the urge to rub at his shoulder, though it began to throb in the presence of so much telumium.

Louisa's eyes widened with a sudden understanding. "They're adding it to the munitions to make them even more devastating."

He swore, imagining the whole Hapsburg army equipped with powerful incendiary devices. Anyone who opposed them would be destroyed. The British Fleet would be wiped from the sky, and ground forces would be leveled.

"Time to plant our own explosives," he growled.

She moved to his back and removed one of the bombs from the improvised pack. After unscrewing the top of the shell, she set the timing device. She set her stopwatch, as well. Once she was satisfied, she replaced the shell's top and hid the whole object between two racks.

"Takes care of one," she said.

"Two left."

"And a ticking clock."

After shutting off her quartz lantern, they hurriedly left the storage room. Louisa continued to lead the way, darting up a staircase. He took the steps four at a time, and met her at the top of the stairs. She threw him a glance that tried to look unimpressed by his athletic display, but she couldn't quite hide the appreciation in her gaze.

A thick door stood on the landing. Even with this barrier, it couldn't dampen the sound of clanging metal on the other side. He cautiously opened the door, and they both stepped out onto a catwalk.

The catwalk ran around the perimeter of a huge chamber. Hissing steam pipes and heavy girders traversed the ceiling. Below was a scene out of an industrial fantasia. Giant sheets of metal were being run through enormous machines, where they were stamped into different-sized shells. Men and women operated the machines, everyone wearing canvas clothing, their shoes soled with felt to keep from generating dangerous sparks, the women tucking their long hair into caps so it wouldn't be caught in the machinery.

All along the plant floor were munitions in states of manufacture, from their raw components to final assembly. At the farthest end of the assembly room, workers mixed chemicals to form the explosive charges. Next to them, more workers packed the explosive materials into the formed shells. Close to where Christopher and Louisa stood, workers racked completed munitions into more crates, which were loaded onto wheeled platforms and carted away by clanking automatons.

Even with the mechanized workers, the munitions plant employed hundreds, if not a thousand, men and women.

"We can't kill these people," he said to Louisa. They might build weapons to be used against the British, but they were only trying to earn a living.

"Never my intent," she answered. "I've a plan that will not only spare their lives, but will help get us out undetected. But we have more work to do before then."

They hurried along the catwalk, careful to keep out of sight of anyone on the factory floor. Armed guards were stationed below at intervals, but the sentries looked bored, one even yawning into the cuff of his jacket.

Heavy support girders crossed the width of the factory, supporting many of the machines that handled the dangerous materials. Louisa stopped beneath a central girder.

"We bring this one down, the whole chamber will collapse." She took another bomb from his pack, cradling it in her arms. "Give us a boost." She eyed the girder overhead.

"I'll go," he said at once.

"Who do you think they'll notice less? A big Man O' War in his naval uniform or a thoroughly nondescript woman?" Before he could answer, she said, "Either help me up, or I'll find a way up on my own. And the more time you argue, the more time we lose." She locked her gaze with his. "Trust me, Kit."

He exhaled, then interlaced his fingers, forming a stirrup.

She gave him a brief nod and set her foot into the cradle of his hands. In one motion, he hoisted her up. She set the bomb on the metal beam and then climbed onto the girder on her hands and knees. Once she had gained her position, she slowly stood, her arms wrapped around the bomb. For a moment, she swayed, adjusting her equilibrium to accommodate carrying the explosive device. Satisfied with her balance, she began to walk out on the girder.

His breath refused to leave his body as he watched her progress. With a delicate, acrobatic grace, she walked along the support beam. Her steps took her over the factory floor, some forty feet below. If she fell, not only would she be detected, but she'd go crashing into brutal machinery that would crush her.

Though her steps were careful and slow, she showed no fear or reluctance. Only walked on, her gaze downcast to track her progress.

Somehow, a loose bolt had wound up on the girder. She might step on it and stumble, or else kick it and send it clattering down, attracting disastrous attention.

Damn it. He had to warn her. But if he shouted, he'd be heard by the people below.

But Louisa was no amateur. She stepped carefully over the bolt. Her skirts didn't even brush against it as she passed.

He still couldn't exhale. Staying back in the less-illuminated part of the catwalk, he watched as she set the bomb down at the very center of the support beam, opened it and set the timer, replaced the top, then started her return journey. Again she avoided knocking the loose bolt to the ground, and headed quickly toward the catwalk. Without the burden of the bomb, she went much faster, moving with an elegant agility.

He took a breath only when her steps took her back over the catwalk. He reached up to assist her in dismounting, but she swung down on her own, dropping lightly to her feet.

"Prettier than any waltz I've ever seen," he said.

Her eyes seemed to glow, and he couldn't fault her for looking pleased with herself. He couldn't have been more impressed. Grinning, she said, "A hell of a lot more useful, too."

Neither of them wanted to test their luck by lingering. They hurried along the catwalk until they reached the other end of the manufacturing room. Hastening through another door, they came to a stairwell leading four stories down. She ran down them quickly, but he decided he would move faster.

He leapt over the railing to the stairs just below, then vaulted over the next railing to the stairs beneath that. Two more times he repeated the process, swiftly making short work of the staircase and passing Louisa along the way.

They reconvened at the bottom of the stairwell.

"Now you're just showing off," she said with a shake of her head.

"It's working. Look how dazzled you are."

Their brief humor vanished, however, as they continued on their mission. He was conscious of time slipping away and the continual presence of danger all around. As they crept through more corridors, several times they had to duck into alcoves or behind support beams to avoid being spotted by sentries. Hiding his considerable size wasn't easy, and it went against his very nature to shrink away from a threat, but the last thing he wanted was a firefight inside a munitions plant. Especially with Louisa by his side.

They slipped down a passageway, then stopped outside another closed door. She tried the handle.

"Damn. Locked." From her pack, she produced a small velvet case. A series of picks were lined up inside—the tools of a thief. Or spy.

It would be so easy for him to kick the door down. Easy, and satisfying. All the exertions of the mission had barely burned the energy seething within him. But he forced himself to stand and wait patiently as she worked the lock with her picks.

She gave him a wink as the lock tumbled into place, and the door swung open.

Within this chamber were stacked countless barrels and glass jars. He inhaled and caught the sour odors of saltpeter and sulfur, and sharp chemical scents.

"The raw ingredients for the explosives are stored in this series of rooms," she said. "Components for gunpowder and trinitrotoluene."

Making it an ideal location for the third and final bomb.

He pulled off his pack and removed the bomb himself before handing it to Louisa. She placed it against one of the walls and set the timing device.

"The blast will knock out the walls," she said as she worked, "mixing the components."

"They'll combine," he deduced, "and then all of these chambers turn into one giant bomb."

After she replaced the top of the bomb's shell casing, she checked her pocket watch once more. "Thirty minutes, then all three detonate."

"It'll take us more than half an hour to get out of here without being seen." They might have made a full-out run for it, but that would have meant drawing the attention of the guards and likely winding up in a firefight—a consequence to be avoided.

"That's already been considered."

She strode out to the corridor, Christopher following, and hurried over to a small glass-fronted case mounted on the wall, the word *Incendiu* painted on it. A lever was behind the glass. Picking up the little brass hammer hanging by a chain, she smashed it into the glass. Then pulled the lever.

A tremendous ringing filled the corridor.

At once, people poured out of rooms wearing looks of panic. They shouted and shoved as they barreled in one direction. None of them noticed the English Man O' War in their midst, nor looked twice at Louisa's unfamiliar face. They were too concerned with getting out of the munitions plant.

His arm around Louisa's shoulders, he allowed himself to go with the throng, pushed along as though being propelled by a surging tide. They bustled through the main assembly room, past half-completed munitions and un-thinking automatons still pushing loaded pallets. More and more workers joined the fleeing crowd. Even the armed guards had abandoned their posts and ran for the exit.

Though chaotic, he had to admit this was a damn sight faster way to leave the plant. And it gave him and Louisa ample camouflage.

Up ahead shone daylight. The front entrance doors had been flung open, and workers poured out, running for safety. He'd never been so glad to see the sun as when he and Louisa crossed the threshold, emerging into open air. The workers must have been drilled for the possibility of a fire, for they all crossed the open expanse outside the factory and headed toward the right, in the direction of the train tracks.

Exultation flared in his chest, but he beat it back. The mission was ongoing. Nothing was certain.

Not true. One thing *was* certain. They needed to reach the woods, where the jolly boat would meet them. Which meant that they had to separate themselves from the evacuating workers, undoubtedly drawing the guards' attention. And they needed to do it at once. Minutes were slipping by, and the bombs would explode soon.

He took Louisa's hand. Together, they ran across the cleared plain surrounding the plant and sped toward the forest. As they ran, he pulled the flare gun from his belt and fired it into the air. The flare arced up with a whine and a streak of light.

Shouts sounded behind them. Then came the pop of gunfire and shriek of bullets piercing the air. Chunks of dirt and rock flew up from the ground as bullets hit the ground. No time to stop and return fire.

Louisa gasped as he scooped her up in his arms, never breaking stride. Confident that he had her in a secure hold, he unleashed his fullest speed, tearing toward the shelter of the woods.

He darted between the trees with her in his arms. Bullets slammed into tree trunks, the force of the ether rifles' ammunition turning them into splinters. Louisa pulled her ether pistol and shifted in his arms, bracing her forearms on his shoulders and firing back at the guards. The pursuing men yelled to one another, and he could hear them fall back slightly, held off by her covering fire.

They stopped at the edge of a clearing, and he set her down. Using the trees for cover, they continued to return fire, keeping the advancing soldiers at bay as they waited for the jolly boat.

A hum sounded overhead, and a shadow crossed the clearing. The jolly boat descended into the glade. Josephson manned the swivel gun at the prow, holding back the guards as Christopher and Louisa ran for the boat.

Both he and Louisa leapt into the vessel.

"Go!" he shouted to Farnley.

The words had barely left his mouth when the jolly boat rose up, heading for the safety of the sky. More bullets tore through the air around them.

As the jolly boat flew higher, Louisa was already out of his arms and returning fire, with Josephson on the mounted swivel gun. Christopher hefted a rifle from the boat's supply and lay down a barrage of bullets. He made certain to wing the enemy shooters, ensuring they couldn't use their weapons.

Farnley shouted above the tumult, "Bad news, sir. Hun patrol ships found us. *Demeter*'s been ducking and weaving as much as she can, but it's only a matter of time till it's a full engagement."

Lowering his rifle, Christopher glanced up and swore. He'd been preoccupied with getting away from the munitions plant—too distracted to notice that his airship barely stayed out of the sights of the enemy's fire. A pitched battle was about to be fought just over his head, the *Demeter* on the verge of taking a beating from Hapsburg ether cannons.

The jolly boat found itself navigating the dangerous air between the *Demeter* and the pursuing Hapsburg ships. Taking the tiller away from a grateful Farnley, Christopher guided the small boat through the hail of cannon and gunfire. They'd left the forest, and firing guards, far below.

The jolly boat dipped and wove as he avoided the volley of gunfire. A bullet slammed into the hull. Another whizzed dangerously close to Josephson's head.

The *Demeter*'s cargo doors were open, ready to receive the jolly boat. He fought to position the boat while also avoiding enemy fire, the process like threading a needle in the middle of a battlefield. But he needed to be on his ship. He must command his crew.

He brought the jolly boat up through the cargo doors.

The moment the doors closed, he was out of the boat, Louisa beside him.

The ship quaked from the force of a narrowly avoided broadside. Pullman's yelled orders rose above all this.

Christopher leapt up the stairs, shouldering past crew. He heard Louisa behind him, following as quickly as she could.

He reached topside. Though the *Demeter* had managed to avoid most of the enemy's barrage, cannon smoke hung thickly in the air. Hapsburg Gatling guns made a continual *chop-chop-chop* above shouts and gunfire.

Pullman hurried over the moment Christopher emerged on deck. "Thank God you made it, sir."

"Just in time to get torn from the sky," he answered, grim. Several crewmen lay on the deck. One wasn't moving. The others groaned and writhed from their wounds. With an open bag of tools and supplies beside him, Dr. Singh and his assistant attended to the injured men.

Three Hun airships attempted to surround them—the *Kühnheit* and two others. He could see their Man O' War captains—men as large as Christopher, wearing Hapsburg crimson and blue—pacing back and forth across their decks, issuing commands. Each of the enemy ships had turned its guns on the *Demeter*, and only her evasive maneuvering had kept them safe. But she couldn't dance forever.

"Awaiting your orders, sir," said Pullman. "Shall I tell the venters to make ready? We can try to outrun the enemy."

"Not yet."

"Sir?" The ship gave another shudder.

"We're not running. We're fighting. Fighting back."

The nearby crew heard this and grinned, eager to spill Hapsburg blood after the enemy had wounded fellow crewmen.

"Engage with that ship," Christopher ordered, nodding toward the *Kühnheit*. "We'll use their own ship as a barrier. If we keep it between us and the other Hapsburg airships, they won't be able to fire on us, not without the possibility of hitting one of their own."

He turned to the men manning the ship's armaments. "Four-inch guns, soften up the enemy's sides. Same with the Gatling guns. Fourteen inchers, I want you aiming for their ether tanks."

"The central tank is the most critical," Louisa added. "The other two tanks are back-up, but they don't have as much buoyancy."

"You heard the lady," he shouted to his crew. "Shoot for the central tank."

"Do we hold our position, sir?" asked Pullman.

"Have Mr. Dawes back us toward the munitions plant."

"Back, sir?"

Christopher fixed the first mate with a look. Immediately, Pullman ran to relay the command to the helmsman.

The *Demeter* finally unleashed her firepower, guns booming. For a moment, the enemy ships didn't return fire, as if stunned that their prey was putting up a fight.

That stunned moment didn't last. Hapsburg guns roared back to life.

Christopher turned to Louisa. "How much time until the bombs detonate?"

She pulled out her watch. "Five minutes."

He nodded. That should give them enough time.

"Keep using that Hun ship as a blockade," he shouted to Dawes.

He and Louisa stood at the rail, giving them a view of the Hapsburg airships firing on the *Demeter*. The enemy strove to avoid her guns and breach the distance between the airships. He knew the ships' captains believed that they stalked their quarry. Heavy smoke clotted the air, and the lowering sun turned the smoke bright orange and gold, as though the sky itself burned.

Once the *Demeter* was above the plant, he shouted to the helmsman, "Lower, Mr. Dawes. I want us no more than a thousand feet over that factory. And venters, stand by for my command."

"Aye, sir," came the responses.

The airship sank, getting closer to the munitions plant. The enemy ships followed, maintaining their bombardment as the *Demeter* slid from side to side, firing when she could and avoiding taking direct hits. Far below, the workers from the plant had abandoned the factory and picked their way across the train bridge to collect at the edge of the distant forest.

Louisa studied the munitions plant through her spyglass. "Guards are going back into the factory. We hid the bombs well, but the guards might find them."

"Not in time, they won't."

"Kit," Louisa said warningly. "We have to go."

"Quiet. We played your game down there. We're in the sky now, and it's my rules." He plucked the watch from her hand.

One minute to go.

With Christopher continuing to issue orders, telling which guns when and where to fire, the *Demeter* fought like a tigress, her crew refusing to back down as they threw back salvo after salvo. All the while, Dawes ensured that the *Kühnheit* blocked the other enemy ships. The helmsman also continued to back the *Demeter* up toward the mountain. Christopher would be sure that Dawes got a special commendation. If they survived.

Forty-five seconds. Thirty.

The mountain was at the *Demeter*'s aft. Three Hapsburg ships closed in.

"We're cornered," Louisa said darkly.

"I need you to be my timekeeper," he said, handing her back her watch. Then, louder he called, "Venters, on my command." He grabbed the nearby shipboard auditory device. "Brace yourself and grip your bollocks tight, men."

"Twenty seconds," Louisa said. "And I don't have bollocks."

"You can hold onto mine."

The enemy ships fired again, narrowly missing the *Demeter*. Pieces of the mountain behind them shattered.

There was nowhere else to run. The next barrage wouldn't miss its mark.

"Ten," said Louisa.

"Venters, now!"

"Five. Four."

There was a shudder and hiss, and then the *Demeter* shot forward. Her keel scraped against the top of the *Kühnheit*. Glancing down, Christopher saw the captain of the enemy ship watching the *Demeter* speed past. The Hapsburg Man O' War cursed and shouted orders at his men.

The enemy ships began to turn to pursue.

"Three," Louisa called above the rushing wind. "Two. One."

The ship quaked. Christopher looked back to see a massive fireball tearing through the munitions plant as thousands of pounds of explosives detonated, tearing through solid stone. He could feel its heat, its percussive force, in the very marrow of his bones. Louisa raised her hand, shielding her eyes from the glare. The giant explosion barely missed the *Demeter's* stern.

A huge black cloud billowed up into the sky, obscuring the enemy ships.

The cloud thinned, revealing the Hapsburg airships. They moved slowly, listing and spinning.

They hadn't been as fortunate as the *Demeter*. Debris from the explosion had torn through their keels. One ship had her main ether tank shattered. Giant holes gaped in their hulls. All three limped away from the still burning munitions plant, then, one by one, they sank down, slowly, inexorably snapping trees as they lowered to the ground.

Throngs of factory workers began to gather around the downed ships. There would be no pursuit.

The *Demeter* wheeled quickly in the sky and disappeared over the mountain ridge, hiding their fleeing path. No one would be able to report their course to higher authorities.

Relief and triumph surged through him, as though currents of built-up energy within had finally been released.

"It worked." Louisa sounded shocked.

He pulled her close and kissed her. Hard. They were still alive, and he held her in his arms—he couldn't figure which was the greatest miracle.

Neither, he decided, as he tasted her—gunpowder and jasmine. Miracles were for the passive, the helpless. Two words he'd never use to describe himself, or her. Together, they had fought every step of the way.

Chapter Twelve

LOUISA STOOD AT the window of Christopher's quarters. The night sky over Greenwich bloomed with fireworks, a profusion of fiery color to herald the victorious return of the *Demeter*. Faintly, Louisa heard the blare of a marching band comprising both people and automatons. A full-scale celebration in honor of the *Demeter*'s service and the destruction of the enemy's key munitions plant.

Christopher was down there. So was most of the crew. Accepting their commendation, as was their due.

As a member of Naval Intelligence, she couldn't join them. The press would be there, with their cameras and illustrators. Besides, the work of a spy was never given public acclaim. Nor even private approbation. At best, she might receive a handshake and quiet, gruff words of praise. No medals. No honors. It didn't bother her. Her motivations had never been about glory.

Still, it felt a little lonely, all the way up in the ship, everyone else below. The *Demeter* was quiet as the skies around her filled with cheerful mock explosions. She'd dimmed the lamps in his quarters to see the fireworks better, and the cabin turned crimson, gold, and blue in turns.

Where was Christopher down there? Surrounded by the Admiralty, shaking hands, or taking thumps on the back from the most senior-ranking officers? The fireworks offered intermittent light, and she hadn't his extraordinary eyesight. So she could only assume he was milling through the crowd, giving his statement to the press. Receiving the acclaim that was justly his.

She would wait until the celebration was over before heading to her flat in Knightsbridge. Safer, quieter that way. And . . . she wasn't eager to leave the ship. To return to her life. There was too much unresolved between her and Christopher. And if she slipped away now, while he was busy at the festivities, he might think she was running again.

So she remained on the airship, watching the jubilation below. As she observed the fireworks display and the crowds milling around the airfield, she thought of the week that had passed as the *Demeter* had made her way back to England. It had taken over a day at top speed for the ship to reach neutral airspace. Not an easy feat with the amount of damage the *Demeter* had sustained.

Repairs had been hastily done. The four crewmen who'd lost their lives during the battle over the munitions plant were laid to rest. That had been a hard day. The ship had hovered inches above the Adriatic, and the caskets were lowered into the sea. The crew stood solemn in the face of death.

Christopher had read from the *Book of Common Prayer* and also a passage from Ada Lovelace.

"'I never am really satisfied that I understand anything,'" he had read, "'because, understand it well as I may, my comprehension can only be an infinitesimal fraction of all I want to understand.'"

With respect paid over the watery graves, the ship had then headed for home.

She'd spent her time typing her report on a compact typewriter borrowed from Dr. Singh and investigating every inch of the ship. Though Christopher had hoped she might take her leisure, she couldn't be idle. She drew diagrams and made notes about the working of the airship, eager to learn all her secrets. Her days were full of information.

And her nights had been pleasant. More than pleasant. Wondrous. She and Christopher had made love for hours, rediscovering each other, learning new truths. Sometimes they were a tempest, other times a zephyr.

Even with the passion between them bright, there were questions, so many questions, all of them unasked and unanswered.

During a prowl of Christopher's quarters, she had discovered a single glove tucked into the back of his toiletries kit. A woman's glove, made of pale yellow kidskin, its buttons sparkling beads of jet. Jealousy flared, until she recognized it as one of her own. She hadn't seen its mate in, what, three years?

The glove had looked far more worn, its leather even more supple, than she remembered. It had been a fairly new pair when she'd lost the left glove. Which meant he must have held it, run his thumb over the soft kidskin. In this very cabin, he'd done this.

That glove was now in her pocket. She felt its presence like a ghost of herself as she continued to watch the celebration.

Footsteps sounded in the passageway outside. The cabin door opened.

She turned, surprised, as Christopher stepped into his quarters, shutting the door behind him.

He wore his dress uniform, an acre of navy wool, gold epaulets and gleaming brass, dress sword buckled at his side. She'd seen many dress uniforms, but only his made her heart kick and her breath come faster.

"You're supposed to be down there."

"Didn't care for the company." He set his cap down on a table and strode across the cabin, straight to her. "The person I wanted beside me wasn't there."

Oh, there went her heart again. Thumping harder than the drum below.

She dipped her hand into her pocket and pulled out the yellow glove.

They both stared at it. He took the glove from her and ran his thumb over it, finger by finger, as though following familiar paths.

"All this time," she murmured. "Even when you hated me. You kept it."

"Couldn't throw it away." His voice was a low rumble. "I tried. More than a few times. I never could."

"At my flat in Knightsbridge, I've a box, about this

big." She held her hands twelve inches apart. "Full of keepsakes, reminders. Anyone would think them bits of haphazard debris. A Kentucky cheroot, half-smoked. A linen napkin stained with red wine. A little clockwork butterfly, missing one of its wings."

"The cheroot we shared on the roof of Headquarters. That café in Brighton, when the shop girls on holiday knocked into our table and spilled the wine. And the memento they gave away at the Mechanical 20th Fair. The wing fell off almost immediately."

As he spoke, she felt something huge and bright fill her, something so immense she thought she couldn't possibly contain it. Yet she did. It swelled within her and made her as radiant as hope itself.

She took his hand. "I love you, Kit. I want us to be together again."

Her heart continued to pound. Its throb filled her ears, drowning out the fireworks, as she waited for his answer.

He was silent for a long time. And in his silence, she had her answer. The bright enormity within her curled at the edges. She started to pull her hand away.

Suddenly, she was in his arms.

His mouth was ravenous for hers, and she shared his hunger as they kissed. Tremors wracked his big body and her own smaller form.

"I love you, Lulu." He traced his lips along her neck in patterns of need and heat.

She exhaled, a long, slow, thorough breath that was both a release and an expansion. "All it took was defying death."

He cupped her head with his hands, his gaze intent on hers. "I knew before then. I've always loved you." His eyes darkened. "Thinking of my life without you . . ." He shook his head. "I've been a sailor, a captain of a seafaring ship, then a captain in Her Majesty's Aerial Navy. But I'm so much more when I'm with you."

They kissed again, and the thought came to her, as clear as if she'd spoken aloud. *This is happiness.*

But it wasn't complete. Not until she'd finished what she needed to say.

"Marry me, Kit."

He pulled back to stare at her, and the hot, dark pleasure in his eyes stole thought. Yet he said, "You don't have to—"

"I *want* to. I want you. I want us, together. Forever." She offered him a tremulous smile. "As you said, there may be changes, but they'll be good changes."

He frowned. "There's fear in your eyes."

"All adventures have an element of fear in them. That's what makes them worthwhile." She stroked her fingers across the high contours of his cheekbones, the face of the man who knew her with such profound intimacy. "Let's take this adventure together."

She let her heart show in her gaze, opening herself fully to him. No hiding. No running away.

He kissed her again. Deeply. Then, "Yes. I'll marry you."

She thought she'd felt happiness moments earlier. Now . . . now she thought she might shatter into a million glittering fragments like the pyrotechnics outside.

"Before you accept my acceptance," he said, concern tightening his expression, "there are two things you need to know."

Unease plucked at her. "The first?"

"I can't give you children. Man O' Wars are sterile. The heat we generate . . ." He looked grim. "If you marry me, you won't be a mother."

The knot of anxiety loosened in her chest. "I only want you, Kit. And I'll have you without a single regret."

The concern in his gaze lessened. But did not disappear. "The other thing—you know I can't be away from my ship. Perhaps for a few days, but it wouldn't be like when I was at sea and could be home for months. If we marry, I cannot make a home with you on land. My life's in the sky now."

"Then the sky will be my home, too." She loved the hope in his eyes, and the fact that he would deprive her of nothing. "I know that you are the *Demeter* are inseparable. Fortunately, I'm such a generous woman that I'm willing to share you. On our journey back to England, I thought about our domestic arrangements. I've hit upon the perfect solution."

She stepped from his arms and drifted backward, toward the bed. As she walked, she began to undo the buttons of her blouse. He watched the movements of her fingers, attentive as a hawk.

"We're great heroes," she said, "us and the *Demeter*'s crew. That's what the celebration down there is all about. Thanks to our efforts, the Eastern Front has finally turned. Britain has a better chance of winning the war.

Which means," she continued, slipping off her blouse, "that the Admiralty owes us a rather great favor." She pulled off her boots, then undid the fastenings of her skirt. It slid down, until she stood in her chemise, corset, and pantalets.

Carved lean with desire, he stalked toward her, shedding his own clothing as he moved. He shed his dress sword first, and it hit the ground with a heavy, metallic thud. There were many buttons on his dress coat, and he undid them all. "What is this great favor?"

"I'll continue my work for Naval Intelligence from the unique vantage of an airship. From the *Demeter*, specifically. My survey was very thorough, so I already have a head start. Doubt anyone in Intelligence has the knowledge that I do." She undid her corset and dropped it to the ground, then stepped out of her pantalets.

"You can liaise with a Man O' War. One-on-one." His beautiful dress uniform was scattered across the cabin—coat, waistcoat, shirt, boots, and breeches. He wore only his drawers, and these he peeled off, revealing him in his proud animal nudity. He was hard and eager for her. The bright explosions from the fireworks gleamed along his implants and in the crystalline blue of his eyes.

"A unique opportunity to work very closely with a Man O' War." Her chemise joined the other clothing upon the floor. They were both naked now, in every way.

"They can't refuse that request," he said. "I won't allow them to."

Ah, there was that unconquerable will of his, shaping the world to fit his demands.

He deftly scooped her up in his arms and laid her down upon the bed, then stretched out beside her.

"It won't be the most traditional marriage," she murmured, stroking her fingers over the planes of his chest, feeling his heart beat in time with her own. "But we've never been traditional, you and I."

"A very modern couple," he agreed.

Her hand stilled. "Do you mind—saying it again?"

He knew precisely what she wanted to hear. "I love you. From the moment you showed me your legs on the balcony, I've loved you."

She couldn't stop her laugh, and it felt so good, to laugh with him again. There would be more of that, more laughter, more danger—he was a Man O' War, after all, and made for battle—and she welcomed all of it.

"I love you, Kit. I can't wait to have more adventures with you."

He gave her his wide, brilliant grin. "You and me, sailing the skies together. The world has no idea what's coming. I almost feel sorry for it."

"Almost."

"Not enough to let you go."

"And I'm not letting *you* go. Never again."

They drank deeply of each other. Outside, in a shower of light, fireworks cast countless stars into the sky.

**If you loved *Skies of Fire*,
watch for the next installment in
the smart, sexy Ether Chronicles collaboration
. . . this time set in the American West
and written by Nico Rosso . . .**

U.S. Army Upland Ranger Tom Knox trades the front lines for a different conflict as he returns home to California on his ether-borne mechanical horse. Two years ago, he skipped town, leaving the one girl who ever mattered. Rosa Campos. He thinks she'll be settled down but discovers Rosa's the town sheriff, caught in a battle with a mining company's three-story, rock-eating machine. Tom's the last person Rosa expects to see riding out of the sky to her aid, and seeing him again reignites a flame more dangerous than the enemy threatening to destroy them both.

**Coming July 2012
from
Avon Impulse**

About the Author

ZOË ARCHER is a RITA® Award–nominated author who writes romance novels chock-full of adventure, sexy men, and women who make no apologies for kicking ass. Her books include The Hellraisers paranormal historical series and the acclaimed Blades of the Rose paranormal historical adventure series. She enjoys baking, tweeting about boots, and listening to music from the '80s. Zoë and her husband, fellow romance author Nico Rosso, live in Los Angeles. Visit her website at www.zoearcherbooks .com.

Be Impulsive!

Look for Other
Avon Impulse Authors

www.AvonImpulse.com